When

What got his initial attention back at the store was the regal way she tilted her head, the straightness of her stance, her full chest, small waist and the inviting sway of her hips. Then she had laughed and he was hypnotized, unable to stop looking at her. Now, as he held her close, Winston decided that the look in her eyes was just as hypnotizing.

When Dreams Float

by

Dorothy Elizabeth Love

Indigo Love Stories

Indigo Love Stories
An imprint of Genesis Press Publishing

Genesis Press, Inc.
315 Third Avenue North
Columbus, MS 39701

When Dreams Float
ISBN: 158571-104-7
Manufactured in the United States of America
First Edition

Visit us at www.genesispress.com
or call at 1-888-Indigo1

Dedication

To my nephew and his wife, Spurgeon and Lakeshia—
Continue to seek the happiness you have found...I love you both.

To my Readers—

Everlasting Moments and *When Dreams Float* are both novels in my TLC "Travel and Love Collection," which means the novels are designed to cuddle your senses. Each novel in this line will feature an exotic, romantic place. *Everlasting Moments* was set in Rio de Janeiro. The one you're about to read, *When Dreams Float,* is a romantic comedy set in Tahiti—a place I can't wait to go back to. This is a special treat for you. Cuddle up and enjoy!

1

If there was ever a time to thank his lucky stars, this was it.

But Winston Knight was a man of science and didn't put much stock in chance or luck. He dealt better with facts. And the fact of the matter was that something about her halted him, excited his insides and numbed him to the world around him. He didn't understand why he felt so drawn to her, and that intrigued him.

Another luscious thought ricocheted through Winston's mind as he watched her slip the long gold chain around her neck, its attached pendant dipping between the pale yellow lace of her blouse. The pendant lay softly against cinnamon brown skin. How he would love to run his fingers up, down and around that chain.

The problem was he had never met her before. And from where he was standing on the other side of the jewelry store, he wouldn't get the chance. She was about to leave.

Somewhere in his aroused fog a voice called to him. "Final call for Flight Number TN1 to Papeete, Tahiti."

Winston quickly glanced down at his watch. He was booked on that flight, the start of his business trip, a medical retreat. It was the only plane leaving Los Angeles airport for Papeete this afternoon. His mind warred between rushing to catch his flight or missing it in order to go around the jewelry shop counter and confront the attractive lady who had caused his current physical condition.

Making a quick decision Winston took a step in her direction, stopping only long enough to put back the item he'd picked up to use as an excuse to stare at the woman as she had tried on the necklace. He had never had an immediate reaction this strong and was dying to discover more. He would end this fantasy and go introduce himself.

Maybe this won't start as another mundane business trip after all, he thought. "Damn it!" he mumbled looking around the store. "Where did she go?"

Entering the corridor, he looked to the left, away from his plane and saw a figure dressed in pale yellow amongst a crowd of people headed around a corner. He looked to the right and saw the airline attendant preparing to close the gate to his plane. Even if he sprinted like a NFL running back, he wouldn't make it to his dream girl in time to still make the flight.

"Damn," he said, reluctantly trotting toward his gate. That would teach him to hesitate before going after something he wanted.

As he boarded the plane, he spotted Chuck Rogers, a friend and fellow doctor. He waved, genuinely glad to see him. He and Chuck had been planning this trip for months. And he was glad to get it started. Besides, the past twenty-four hours had been more taxing than he had expected. His ex-girlfriend, Daphne, had called him last night to argue about his decision to make the trip without her. It had ruined his evening. And the disappointment he had just experienced from missing a chance to meet someone new didn't help much. So Chuck's friendly face was just what he needed.

"Glad you made it. I was getting worried that you wouldn't," Chuck said over the general chatter of travelers and movement in first class. "Where're you sitting?"

Winston glanced at his boarding pass. "Seat 3C. Aisle." He found his seat and placed his carry-on luggage in the overhead compartment.

"I think this one is empty." Chuck pointed to the seat next to him. "Join me back here."

As Winston removed his luggage from overhead someone, he assumed the flight attendant, asked, "Is there an extra blanket under your case?"

"I'm about to remove my bag. I'll check." He took a step backward and bumped into her. Turning to apologize, he felt a jolt, partly from the contact, but mostly from the shock.

An inviting smile greeted him first. Then he noticed the fullness of her ruby-colored lips, the soft slant of her chocolate eyes, the shine of her black hair that lay on soft brown shoulders. She was lovely. There was a hint of Jasmine, her perfume, in the air.

He was definitely the lucky one.

"No." Winston had to think hard to remember the reason she stood next to him. He liked her smile, treasured her closeness. "Yellow looks good on you." His eyes traveled farther down. "Especially with that necklace you have on."

2

"Thank you," she said, fingering the pendant between her thumb and index finger. "I just got this. I thought it would be a nice going-away present to myself."

"Very nice," Winston said, enjoying watching the pendant drop.

He stared at her lovely features before deciding on doing a few things. "Where're you seated? Since there aren't any extra blankets in here, I'll have the flight attendant bring you one."

"Don't worry. I'll probably see one of them around the same time you would since I'm seated next to you."

"3B?" he asked hopeful, not even attempting to hide his smile.

"No. My friend, Sandra, is seated there. I'm at the window in 3A."

Winston turned to his friend. "Chuck, I'll chat with you later," he said, giving him a wink. Chuck smiled; winked back.

"Melanie?" A female voice coming up behind Winston said, "I found another blanket in the back. As much as you fly, I can't believe you packed your jacket in your stowaway luggage."

So her name was Melanie, Winston thought, returning his carry-on bag to the overhead bin. He had an eight-hour plane ride with one seat between him and getting to know a lot more about Melanie. The disappointment at having missed the opportunity to meet her in the jewelry store was soundly replaced by the anticipation of how he was going to make the best of this plane trip. Somehow, he had been given another chance. Twice in one day. He wouldn't strike out.

"Looks like you're taken care of for now," he said.

"I guess I am." She had that alluring smile again.

Winston sat, wondering how he was going to remove Melanie's friend from between them. It would happen before this plane landed, he decided. He wouldn't let Melanie get away until he was sure that ring on her third finger wasn't put there by a boyfriend. It wasn't a wedding ring, so the coast was almost clear. Fate wouldn't be cruel enough to throw the type of curve ball that equaled a loving, gift-giving boyfriend in the mist. If so, that would be strike three. Winston frowned.

There was something in the way she looked up at him, how close she stood in the aisle, that made him think of all sorts of pleasant possibilities. He started having a teenage physical reaction and blamed it on having gone too long without sex. Why else would he react to this woman like this?

Melanie's voice interrupted his thoughts. "Sandra, here's the tourist guide for Tahiti. Maybe we can map out a sightseeing tour?"

"For Pap-pete?" Sandra asked.

"Girl, you're purposely saying that wrong," Melanie said grinning. "The Polynesians pronounce all their vowels. It's Pa-pe-et-a."

"Yeah. There, too." Sandra flipped through the book.

Winston's mind did another calculation. In Papeete, he and Chuck would attend a medical meeting, then take a transport bus to the cruise ship. The ship wasn't scheduled to leave until 10p.m. tonight. That would give him approximately two additional hours in Papeete, depending on how long they were delayed by customs, to learn more about Melanie.

Lord, he thought, if anyone could read his thoughts, he'd be arrested. He hadn't even been introduced to the woman and he was planning the next several encounters with her. With that thought, he decided to change things.

He turned to face them. "Papeete is Tahiti's version of New York." He was looking at Melanie when he finished with, "Lots of fun things to see and do."

"I know it's the capital," Sandra said. As she turned to look at him, her long braids flowed about her dark chocolate shoulders. "I was hoping that meant plenty of big-city fun. "So, you've been to Tahiti before?"

"I would love to travel there once a year." Winston decided vagueness might be more of a benefit than admitting this was his first trip. If they thought he had, he could use that to his advantage. "First time for you, Melanie?"

Melanie did a double take upon hearing her name. Then she smiled, gazing at him, possibly wondering whether or not she had met him before.

"This is the first time for us both," Melanie said. "And you are?"

"Very pleased to see you again." Though that statement was true, it was also a ploy. "I'm Winston."

Sandra looked back between Winston and Melanie. "You two know each other?" she said to Melanie.

"We met just a minute ago on the plane," Melanie said looking at his smile. "And, I remember seeing you in the jewelry store today. But...."

"Jewelry store?" Sandra interrupted. "You mean the guy you were...." she stopped, clamping her mouth shut.

"Were what?" Winston wanted to know.

Just then, the captain inconveniently interrupted with a greeting to the passengers. He came across the intercom system promising a wonderful and eventless flight. A bell tone accompanied the seat belt illumination warning and flight attendants began rushing down the aisles. One stopped to stand in the aisle between them, effectively blocking Winston's view of Melanie's wide smile. He would have to explore Sandra's comment and the thoughts behind Melanie's smile later.

But that smile told Winston everything he wanted to hear but couldn't. She had noticed him in the store. So much so, that she had mentioned it to Sandra. There was definitely not a major player in her life that was of any consequence. At least, and Winston felt right about it, he hoped that's what the smile meant.

As the plane soared toward the heavens, so did Winston's spirits. He leaned his head back and allowed pleasant thoughts to entertain him. Pictures of lace and gold and cinnamon brown skin all being dazzled by his touch danced in his head.

Soon, he thought. *Real, soon. And I'll have plenty of time to find out more about her.*

3

Winston was running out of time.

At the rate he was going he wouldn't have any *time* at all to talk to Melanie. They had been in the air for almost six hours and he hadn't had an opportunity to talk to her since the plane took off. Melanie and Sandra had reclined their seats, turned toward the window and covered up with blankets. Two hours after takeoff lunch was served, but they slept through it. Frustrated, Winston had joined Chuck for lunch in the back row of first class on the other side of the plane. After lunch, Winston read a few chapters of a book while Chuck worked on his laptop.

Later, Chuck had even beaten him at a few hands of cards, because Winston was more interested in looking to see if Melanie was up. Now, he could see Sandra was still sleeping, and Melanie's seat was still pushed back in the resting position.

Enough sleep, Winston thought. As he was trying to figure out just how to wake her, Melanie stood and stepped over Sandra into the aisle. She looked at his empty seat, then up at the occupied sign for the front restroom. Turning she headed toward the back of the plane.

"Excuse me, Chuck," Winston said crawling across his friend.

"Catch her before she gets away," Chuck joked.

"Shut up," Winston said, losing sight of Melanie behind the curtains of the attendants' station. She was headed to the rear restroom. "Chuck, I'm headed back to my seat. See you on the ground."

Winston made his way to his seat, wishing the one next to him were empty so he could invite Melanie to join him. Maybe he could pay the man next to him to go sit with Chuck. Of course, his wife might object to that. But what the hell? Desperate times, desperate measures.

Fueled with a newfound determination, Winston rose and went to the mini-kitchen stationed between premiere class and coach class. The area was large enough to comfortably fit several people, but none of the flight attendants were around. The counters were cleaned, coffee was brewing, and nuts and drinks were sitting on shelves for later serving. Winston opened a Sprite and sipped as he waited.

As Melanie walked passed the station, Winston reached out and lightly grabbed her arm. Slightly startled, she dropped her toothbrush and toothpaste.

"Getting to talk to you requires a direct approach," Winston said as he stooped and retrieved her belongings. "All freshened up?"

"Direct would have been following me into the restroom," she said. "Thanks." She took her things from him.

"Then I'm glad you don't mind my subtleness." Her smile was something he realized he had missed the past few hours. He was glad to see it now. "I had planned to entertain you with my jokes but you fell asleep the minute we took off."

"Sandra and I flew into LA last night. There's a lot to do on a Friday evening in LA. We didn't get to bed until very late, figuring to sleep on the trip over."

"Thereby ruining all my plans," Winston added.

"And just what were these unknown plans?" Melanie asked, widening her smile. She crossed her arms under her bust, unknowingly causing her blouse to pull taut across her full chest. Winston didn't miss any of the view.

"To prove what a great guy I am by offering to show you around Papeete," he said softly, after returning his gaze to hers.

She laughed at that. "Have you ever been around Papeete?"

"No," Winston admitted, "But the great guy part would have proven true and you would have forgiven me for being a lousy tour guide."

She laughed again, a musical sound. Winston found himself entertained by it.

The plane hit some turbulence and the craft pitched from side to side. Melanie stumbled and Winston pulled her toward him. Her empty hand reached for his supporting arm. His hands went around her waist to steady her. He could not only feel the cotton of the full skirt and delicate switching in the lace blouse, but the warmer more scintillating skin between them as the blouse lifted. His fingers marveled at their finding.

Winston concluded that prayers were probably heard more clearly the closer to heaven you were. He had just wished to touch her right before she fell into his arms.

"I'm sorry," she said. "I didn't mean to stumble into you like that."

"Don't," he said, not wanting her to move away.

She was referring to her clumsiness. "Manners. An old habit that makes me apologize when I'm in the wrong."

"Don't move just yet. We might hit another air pocket. You wouldn't want to stumble away from me and break something like... my feelings because of it, and ruin my whole trip."

"You're funny." She laughed again. "And cute up close, but you can turn loose because the plane has stopped bouncing. And I do believe your feelings will be okay."

He took in the shape and details of her mouth as she looked seductively, searchingly up at him. She wasn't smiling, but her mouth tipped up naturally, making her look serenely happy. Two things he hadn't felt in a long while: serenity or happiness.

What got his initial attention back at the store was the regal way she tilted her head, the straightness of her stance, her full chest, small waist and the inviting sway of her hips. Then she had laughed and he was hypnotized, unable to stop looking at her. Now, as he held her close, Winston couldn't decide if that look in her eyes was just as hypnotizing. He didn't want to let go of the feeling of serenity she exuded. But he finally managed to release her and she stepped back.

"May I ask you something?" he finally asked his voice husky.

"I think you'll ask me regardless." Out of the corner of her eye, Melanie could see someone coming down the aisle. She stepped forward, closer, to get out of the way.

Winston read her movement differently than intended. "You're right," he said as he pulled her into his arms. Her expression registered surprise, but she never took her eyes off his as his mouth touched hers. He chanced a taste of her and she tasted of toothpaste and joy and something he couldn't put his finger on, but it made him think of lemons and honey. The latter were part of a remedy he had recommended to many of his patients. For that reason, he concluded that kissing her made him feel better. Hotter. Harder. And it thrilled him.

When she wrapped her arms around him, he moaned softly. Was it a sign of acceptance?

That was something he desperately wanted from her, but didn't realize how much until now. Winston stopped himself from giving in completely to the kiss or else he would be dragging her back to the privacy of a restroom to explore their kiss in greater detail.

Lifting his head he whispered, "I had planned to ask you what you taste like."

"Under the circumstances, you can probably describe that better than I," she managed to respond.

"I think I can."

"And that is?" Her whisper matched his.

"Like a place I've been eagerly waiting to get to."

4

Melanie was about to laugh at that, thinking to tell him the appropriate response was: toothpaste, minty fresh. Or possibly like the honey-flavored candy she had munched on just before deciding to brush her teeth to remove the aftertaste of sleep. But the look on his face, the sound of his voice, the pressure of his hand against her spine all indicated that he wanted her to believe him. And that touched her deep down where she didn't want to have feelings for a man.

She shouldn't have let him kiss her. It was a mistake, she realized a bit too late, but all she had thought about since the moment she had watched him enter the jewelry store was what it would be like to experience him firsthand.

Melanie hadn't noticed him when he had first gotten on the plane because she had been bent over, shoving her large straw bag under the seat in front of her. She had recognized his outfit immediately then somehow found herself standing next to him needing a reason to get his attention. His jeans hugged all the right places, all the right ways. His khaki short sleeve shirt showed off the wonderfully defined muscles of his arms. Arms that held so well, cuddled so nicely, felt so good. And his handsome chocolate face, his full wonderful mouth and warm body were even more overwhelming up close.

Suddenly, the plane pitched again and dipped as the hand of turbulence grabbed the aircraft. The "fasten seatbelts" sign illuminated.

Something about that happening at the end of the kiss added a bit of disbelief to it all. The plane shook again, jarring Melanie back to her senses.

Her blatant response to his kiss should never have happened. If not for the fanciful thoughts she had been having since the moment she had laid eyes on him, it wouldn't have. What started as playful flirtation when he reached for her arm had ended with her losing the game. She wasn't any good at these types of games. And she always got her feelings hurt when she played.

Surely he thought she was an easy lay.

Melanie struggled to think of a way to excuse herself and go hide in her seat. Just then a flight attendant's voice chimed over the intercom, warning all to return to their seats and buckle up.

Any excuse will do, Melanie thought. She needed to escape.

"You both need to return to your seats," an attendant said, walking up to them flashing one of those all-too-fake smiles that probably was taught at flight attendant school.

"Melanie, is the rough movement making you ill?" Winston asked.

"I'm okay," Melanie said, glad to have another reason to walk away from him. She never got seasick or airsick. The pain on her face was actually shame for her actions.

"You don't look okay," Winston said, then turned to the attendant. "Bring extra barf bags to row 3. Let's go, Melanie."

Back at their seats, she was glad to see that Sandra was awake. Another barrier to use to protect her from Winston.

"My God!" Sandra said when she saw them. "I think we're being shot down!"

"It's only turbulence," Melanie said.

"More like turbo," Sandra corrected. "Turbo missiles hitting one of the main engines. I wanted to see the Pacific, but not from 20,000 feet below it!"

"This won't last, Sandra," Winston said, buckling his seat. "Melanie, there should be a bag in your seat pocket if you continue to feel queasy."

"Since when do you get sick on planes?" Sandra asked, looking for her own bag. "Intestinal fortitude runs in your family."

Melanie didn't respond to that, but looked out of the window to avoid Winston's stare.

After what seemed like an hour, but was actually less than ten minutes, the aircraft reached calmer skies. Melanie continued to stare out of the window, watching the pale blue skies turn burnt orange as evening approached this part of the Pacific Rim.

Tahiti time was five hours behind Mountain Time, at her home in Denver. It would be six o'clock when they arrived, eleven at night her body time, yet Melanie was alert and wide awake as thoughts of how she would handle the Winston incident crossed and recrossed her mind.

Winston incident? She smiled on the inside. She was already making it sound like a major ordeal. It was only a kiss that got out of hand with a man she had just met.

Lord. Melanie looked up. Maybe she would awake in an hour and realize she had only been dreaming. She prayed the situation would, or should, correct itself that easily.

"Melanie?" It was Winston's deep voice.

She could pretend to be sleeping, but knew that wouldn't fly because of the five-hour nap she had just taken. She reluctantly turned to face him.

"No regrets today," he said and she nodded her head in agreement.

"Regrets about what?" Sandra wanted to know.

"Doctor-patient privilege," Winston said.

"What doctor?" Sandra was at a complete loss. "What did I sleep through?"

"The ride over," Winston said. "And I'm the doctor."

Melanie and Sandra looked at him in surprise.

The attendant finally showed up with extra barf bags. "For you, Madam?" He gave them to Melanie.

"You sick for real?" Sandra asked in disbelief. "I hate not being in the know!" she whined. "I'm not sleeping another minute on this trip!"

5

A Tahitian evening breeze greeted all one hundred and seventy passengers of Flight TN1 as they climbed down the stairs onto the runway. Tahiti, the largest of the 118 islands and atolls comprising French Polynesia, is in the middle of the Pacific Ocean, just four thousand miles from Los Angeles. Travelers—some tired from jet lag, some not, all showed enthusiasm to finally have made it there. Now they stood wondering, talking and laughing in the custom's lines that started in a covered atrium at a rear entrance to the airport.

The atrium's ceiling fans circulated warm air around the terra cotta entrance that had several large, strangely shaped trees with roots that grew above ground. A band of Tahitian men next to the entrance of the atrium sang rhythmic melodies and played instruments made from wood and bamboo. The band members were adorned with headdresses made from braided palm tree leaves and large scarves worn as skirts. A welcoming committee of women in brightly colored dresses placed wonderfully smelling small white flowers called *Tiare*, the Tahitian gardenia, on the ears of those who passed them.

"Is that a crab?" Sandra asked stopping her frantic search in her oversized purse. In the middle of the atrium, a small land crab negotiated its way through the six caterpillar-slow moving lines of passengers going through customs. "Where the hell is my passport?" Sandra was back to digging in the bag.

"You don't think you left it in LA, do you?" An elderly lady in line behind them asked.

"No," Sandra said in annoyance. "A case of bad packing. I had it on the plane."

"Thank goodness! Bill and I had the same panic just before leaving home," the woman added fanning her tinted reddish-blond hair that did not go far in covering up the gray. "We're from Dallas. And you?"

"I'm from Denver," Melanie said, "Sandra's from Cedar Hills, Texas."

"That's just south of us! I'm Ethel Hightower and this is my husband, Bill." The woman enthused. "It's our fiftieth anniversary and...." she gave a synopsis of the past ten anniversary vacations leading to this trip. They were cruising to countries and islands an ocean at a time. Next year Fuji, another Pacific Ocean island. "Luckily, no poisonous snakes and bugs here. But the mosquitoes...."

If not for the too-long flight, too-warm atrium, and too-disconcerting incident with Winston, Melanie might have enjoyed listening to Mrs. Hightower prattle, non-stop, about their vacation hot spots. Inbred manners forced her to acknowledge the conversation, but she silently prayed for the line to move faster. She hadn't seen Winston since deplaning and hoped it would stay that way. He had gotten off the plane before she and Sandra did, because Sandra had forgotten to complete her custom documents during the flight, and they stayed on the plane so that she could do so. Winston had probably already cleared customs, picked up his luggage and was well on his way to enjoying Papeete.

"Are you married, Dear?" Mrs. Hightower asked Melanie. Sandra wasn't listening.

"No. I'm divorced," Melanie said.

"Too bad," Mrs. Hightower patted her husband on the arm. He stood silently nodding occasionally, more to prove that he was breathing rather than listening. "He couldn't lose me if he tried. With the right man, fifty years is nothing."

"Are you staying in Tahiti or island hopping?" Melanie asked.

"Cruising the islands. They should have these lines by final destination. Some of these people are going to the cruise ships, some are staying here in Tahiti and others are headed to other islands in French Polynesia."

"Nationality is the only way these lines work," Melanie said just to be talking. It was a standard procedure for all custom checkpoints.

"I just don't want to miss my ship. We're traveling on the *Paul Gauguin*. It's one of the smaller cruise ships in the Radisson line, but extremely exclusive nonetheless."

"That's the only way we be travelin'. Exclusive." Sandra purposely added a touch of Ebonics. She never stopped digging for her passport. "We're on the *Paul Gauguin*, too."

"Oh!" Mrs. Hightower looked somewhat deflated, but not deterred. "It's a bit warm today," she changed the subject. "The average temperature is about 79 degrees, but all the islands are like that you know. I had hoped traveling here in March wouldn't be so warm. Mr. Hightower burns so easily. The nice man on the plane next to us, gave us so many great safety tips." She turned in search of something. "Oh, look, Bill." Mrs.. Hightower pointed to the movement at the rear of the line. "It's Dr. Knight. There were a few doctors on our flight. Convention, you know." She began waving him forward. "Bill, he needs to be with us not way back there at the end. The dear man sat with us in first class." Mrs. Hightower lowered her complaint to a secretive tone. "One would think they would have premiere and executive travelers lines for customs…."

Melanie and Sandra had no idea who this Dr. Knight was, but they hoped he would join them quickly to chat with Mrs. Hightower. Melanie was about to suggest she go fetch Dr. Knight herself.

"You'll love meeting him, Dear," Mrs. Hightower said to Melanie. "Has an excellent practice near Highland Park. Treats a lot of the Dallas football players."

The words 'football players' registered in Sandra's brain. "Oh, really!" she quickly chimed, now fully alert to the conversation, and craned her neck around the hoards of people in line behind them.

"It would be nice to chat with him," Melanie said, thinking he would be a great diversion from Mrs. Hightower. But as she stepped around to get a better view, she saw Winston. She quickly moved to stand behind Mr. Hightower, glad for his height. Hopefully Winston wouldn't see her.

"Dr. Knight!" Mrs. Hightower exclaimed. "Join us!"

"Winston?" Melanie looked puzzled.

"Melanie." Winston was smiling.

"Dear, you already know Dr. Knight?"

"I thought you said he was a football player?" Sandra asked.

"Treat football players," Winston corrected.

"Sports medicine?" Melanie asked.

"General practitioner as well," Winston added.

"Ohhh...how nice!" Mrs. Hightower enthused. "All together again."

Melanie prayed that the folks in front of them would hurry up. She couldn't take both Mrs. Hightower and Winston on an empty stomach and with an achy back. She had missed most of the meals on the plane and needed energy to combat them both.

Chuck walked up and Sandra beamed because he looked like a football player.

"Everyone, this is my friend, Chuck Rogers." Winston introduced Melanie, Sandra and the Hightowers.

"Running back or wide receiver?" Sandra asked Chuck excitedly, while attempting to rub wrinkles out of her blue sundress.

"Sorry. I practice medicine, not ball," Chuck corrected.

"What's with all this damn skipping!" The person in line behind the Hightowers shouted at them all. "You can't skip!"

"Medical reunion," Mrs. Hightower explained quickly in a low tone. "We're Dr. Knight's patients." She turned to her husband, "Aren't we, Dear!"

"Doctor, my ass!" The person behind wasn't buying it!

Chuck flashed his medical badge stored inside his passport wallet.

"Heyyyyy," Sandra said, looking for a reason to get closer to Chuck. "Cute passport case. I'm sure you never lose it that way."

"Have you found yours yet?" Mrs. Hightower wanted to know as the line in front of them cleared.

Melanie took advantage and rushed forward. She flashed her passport, impatiently waited for it to be stamped by the inspector, and hurried forward to baggage claim to get her luggage. Luck was on her side; she found her bags immediately. Sandra showed up complaining about the sudden rush as Melanie hurried her along.

"We don't want to miss our bus, Sandra!" Melanie said.

"Fine!" she whined. "But we're stopping for film. I can't find that now."

Just as Melanie was about to wheel her luggage away, Winston stepped in front of her. "Sandra, there's a Duty-free shop over there. They have film. We'll wait for you here."

"Sure thing, Winston." Sandra got a glimpse of another fine brotha walking into the shop. "I just might pick up a few extra things while I'm there."

"Hey again, Melanie," Winston said when they were alone. "I thought we said no regrets."

"Winston, I...." Melanie stopped and took a deep breath. It wasn't like she would ever see the man again. This would be the last time, so what was she running away from? Besides, she had enjoyed the kiss. She had fantasized about him since she first spotted him. And she had hoped to meet someone interesting like him. The least she could do was acknowledge and accept that she had gotten just what she wanted out of this trip so far. "I...." she said truthfully, "I think you're an incredible kisser. And I think you taste like...like 'a good time I wanted to have' and...." she watched his sensual mouth tipped up in a grin. "The flight over was more enjoyable because of you."

She stared at him, taking in all his features. He was tall, muscularly lean, ruggedly handsome man and the shadow of a beard only made his milk chocolate skin even tastier looking. He could easily be charming if he wasn't so arrogant. "This is the last time that we'll ever see each other. Let's just say goodbye."

"Isn't that the name of a great oldies song?" Winston joked.

"Probably," Melanie said. "But it's also a great way for us to part. You're here in Papeete for a meeting. I'm on my way to a ship that won't be back here for a week, when we fly out. So," she exhaled, "have a great time here." She moved to leave but his statement stopped her.

"I would love to help you enjoy your stay."

"I will enjoy it," Melanie affirmed.

"You sure you don't have any regrets?" Winston asked.

"About you?" she looked at his mouth, "Just one."

"And that is?" he asked, intrigued.

"That the turbulence stopped me from kissing you again."

"I think you're flirting with me," he grinned.

"Why not be honest," Melanie smiled. "We won't see each other again."

"You're right," he added. "But we can possibly spend time having fun on your last day, while waiting for the return flight."

"It's a thought, but I'm not the kind of girl you think I am."

"And what kind is that?"

"An easy lay," Melanie told him.

"I never thought you were," Winston said. "I was just suggesting a way we can finish the kiss we started. I like the way you taste."

Like a place I've been eagerly waiting to get to, she remembered him having said that about the way she tasted. Melanie smiled at the memory and took a step toward him. She came up on her toes and pressed her lips to his in a soft, goodbye smooch.

"Bye, Winston," she said.

When she started to step away, he stopped her again. He reached in his pocket and pulled out a business card. "Here's where I am in the U.S. Maybe when we get back to the States you'll change your mind if you're ever in Dallas."

"Maybe."

"You're sure you need to leave now?" Winston asked. "Maybe we can have a drink before you go."

"The *Paul Gauguin* has already started its boarding. Sandra and I need to find the ship, shower and change for the *Bon Voyage* party on board." Melanie saw something that looked like surprise and disappointment in his stare. She guessed he had hoped she would change all her plans to be with him. Her trip was already planned and he wasn't a part of it.

"Enjoy your cruise," Winston said.

"I will," Melanie said.

"Even without me?" he joked.

"I'm sure it would be better with you," she kidded.

"Is that a promise?" he asked.

What the hell, she could flirt. Walking backwards she said jokingly, "You seem like a nice guy; someone who could be quite entertaining. It would be absolutely fantastic if you could be there!" Then she turned to hide her laughter. "But I'll try to manage without you."

He laughed as she waved farewell, then left, not looking back.

Melanie intercepted Sandra and they followed the signs to the *Paul Gauguin* bus transfer station. Winston watched and waved a final goodbye as Chuck came to stand next to him.

"That Sandra is something else," Chuck grinned.

"I was just thinking the same thing about Melanie," Winston said.

"Yeah, but I don't get the impression that Melanie is the freak that Sandra is. She hit on me and some other guy in the Duty-free shop."

"Let's go," Winston said. "We've got to get to that medical check-in meeting."

"I take it you made plans to hook up with Melanie on the Island?" Chuck asked.

"No, she wanted to say goodbye here," he said, "But I found out something else.'

"What's that?" Chuck asked.

"She's on the *Paul Gauguin*."

6

"So, are you going to meet Winston on Bora Bora for some wild and kinky sex?" Sandra asked Melanie as the air-conditioned bus pulled away from Tahiti-Faaa International Airport.

"No."

"Moorea Island then? I think we'll be docked there for two days." Sandra opened her cruise itinerary. "And it's only a thirty-minute motor boat ride from Tahiti."

"Not there, either."

Sandra put down her itinerary and gawked, dropped jaw, in disbelief at her friend. "Whhaaattttt!!????" Sandra placed her hand on Melanie's forehead. "Are you feverish? No," Sandra said, removing her hand, "just plain crazy. The man's fine, intelligent, surely financially secure, and just plain fine!"

"You said the 'fine' part already," Melanie added.

"So where's he staying in Papeete?"

"I'm not sure."

"You're a damn fool," Sandra slapped her itinerary and guidebook in her lap and crossed her arms under her chest. "Why not go after him? Besides, it's been too long since you dated someone."

Melanie liked Sandra's directness. It was a refreshing quality she brought to the friendship. Even though she could be a little abrasive at times, Melanie wasn't offended. "I'm not a fan of casual sex. Especially now that AIDS cases among Black men are climbing. Besides, the divorce isn't that old. Last thing I need in my life is another good-looking guy, especially one who knows it."

"I hope you aren't referring to Ronald, the asshole," Sandra stated. "That was a bad decision and it's in your past. It's been a year."

"My ex was definitely a good-looking cheater and liar, though," Melanie added. "But let's not dwell on his good characteristics." She looked back out the window at the island's beauty. It was extremely clean. Winston was right; Papeete definitely had a big city feel to it. Traffic, streetlights, beautiful homes, shopping malls, City Hall, post office, churches situated throughout the mountains, and all the other comforts, and discomforts, of urban life. And Sandra was probably right as well. Experiencing Winston might have been a good idea.

"Let me give you a little advice." Sandra pulled Melanie back into the conversation. "We're here to have fun. Don't be running off guys I might be interested in. True, I came for a relaxing exotic getaway, and it did help that you got this trip for half the going rate. I say, why go to the over-visited Bahamas, or Hawaii for that matter, when we paid the same price to come here. Hell, I'm looking for the exotic change, but don't go preaching to me about being virtuous."

"You're a nurse," Melanie said. "I'm sure you know how to be safe, sexually and otherwise. I'm not going to preach to you."

"Good, cause I'm not going to pass up on an opportunity for fun! Enough said." Sandra pointed excitedly out of the window. "McDonald's! Feels like home already."

Then so be it, Melanie decided. She would have fun, too! She couldn't wait to get to the ship and start their cruise. And, at least it would give her something else to think about other than letting Winston get away. Maybe she did misjudge him and let an opportunity for fun with him her last day in Tahiti slip by. But he was from Dallas and her friend, Sandra, did live near there. *Who knows*, Melanie thought, *our paths might cross again some day*. "What's the order of the islands we're going to?" Melanie asked Sandra, putting thoughts of Winston and opportunities lost out of her mind.

Opening the itinerary, Sandra read them off: Papeete/Tahiti, Raiatea, Tahaa, the Motu Mahana, Bora Bora, Moorea, then back to Papeete/Tahiti.

"You've gotta get better at pronouncing all of the vowels. It's Ra-I-a-te-a, and Ta-ha-a," Melanie said, laughing.

"Wherever," Sandra joked. "As long as I can stare at fine island men, I'm happy. The language of love needs no vowels."

They both laughed at that.

"I just can't believe you're gonna spend an ounce of time researching these places to write magazine articles."

"It's what I do, Sandra," Melanie said.

"This trip is a good tax write-off for you, is how I see it."

"That, too!" Melanie agreed.

As the bus pulled up to the docks, the *Paul Gauguin* luxury liner looked welcoming. White lights, the Christmas tree variety, lined palm trees that were spread across a large park area next to the docks. Vacationers sat, stood, and lounged all over the area sipping on cool drinks, munching snacks and chatting merrily.

The *Paul Gauguin* was much smaller than the cruise ships Melanie and Sandra had been on before. It slept only 320 people including staff, unlike the ship docked next to it–the type they both were familiar with-which slept thousands. Their ship would leave in a few hours to start the seven-day cruise. Melanie and Sandra skipped the picnic on the docks and headed straight for the ship to shower and change. As they boarded, the cruise director and his staff welcomed them aboard.

A personal server took their carry-on bags. "Right this way," the woman said in a thick French accent. "I'll have everything, including your other luggage carried to your room. I've put fresh fruit, soft drinks and wine in your room. If you want a light snack before the Sail Away Party, the piano bar is on Deck 8."

"Personal server? Oooookkkkkay! Never happened on any ship I've been on," Sandra whispered a bit too loudly. "I'm beginning to feel rich!"

Exotic paintings lined the halls and rooms. The ship was a luxurious tribute to *Paul Gauguin*, the Paris born impressionist painter of the late 1800s. Beautiful reproductions of his art covered the walls.

In 1891, ruined and in debt, Gauguin sailed to the South Seas to escape civilization. Under the influence of the tropical setting and Polynesian culture, his paintings became more powerful, more distinctive and more simplified, and in doing so, changed the status of his life. Tahiti and *Paul Gauguin* became one in the eyes of France, and made him famous.

Melanie entered their majestic stateroom, which featured reprints of several of Gauguin's works, teakwood walls, native stone carvings on shelves and one exotic floral arrangement on a small dining table on the other side of the sleeping area that had two full-size beds. The dining area held a stocked refrigerator and bar on one wall, a loveseat on the other. Over the table was a large window with a wonderful view of mountainous terrain.

Melanie looked around with appreciation and an expectation that this world would inspire her writing as well. "Get a load of this room! I like this smaller ship better. It's more like being on a private yacht than a cruise ship." She moved to the window and looked out over the festivities on the docks. "And those people want to hang around on land? Unbelievable!"

"They gotta be from the other ship. Well, the party starts in an hour," Sandra shouted heading to the bathroom. "Let's hurry and get topside! I don't want to get back off the boat."

"You don't have to tell me twice! Our luggage should be here soon. Then it's sail-away time!"

"Did you see that cute guy in the greeting room!" Sandra called.

"They were all cute," Melanie said. "My goodness, are any of these Polynesian people bad looking?"

"Or short for that matter. Even the women are all tall."

About two hours later, showered, changed and happy to have previously found the restaurant for dinner, Sandra and Melanie sipped Island Delight cocktails, enjoying the live band playing a mixture of jazz, rock, R&B and island music.

"My camera!" Sandra whined loudly. "Tell them to hold the boat. We can't leave until I take pictures of us here!" She jumped up, rushed around the pool, heading back to the room.

Laughing, Melanie exhaled what little worries she had and inhaled the expectation of joy that awaited her over the next seven days. It was going to be a quiet, relaxing good time. Nothing would cause this trip to be anything other than what she had planned. She was sure of it.

"Hey again, Melanie." The deep voice came from behind.

Turning, she almost choked on the sip of her drink. She stood, coughed once to clear her throat, then blinked several times to ensure the alcohol wasn't interfering with her vision.

"Winston?" She managed around a croak. "What are you doing here?"

"Enjoying the sight of you," he said softly.

"No, I mean, on the ship. I thought you said you were going to be in Papeete for a conference or something."

"No," he shook his head. "I said I would give you a tour of Papeete if you wanted me to. We checked-in for the medical conference then Chuck and I came here. The rest of our medical meetings will all be held on this ship."

"*This* ship?" she looked confused. "Vacationers are on this ship."

"The doctors are required to meet every morning for about two hours. Classes, workshops and such," he shrugged. "The rest of the time is ours to enjoy."

"To enjoy?" She said mildly irritated. She wasn't expecting to have her relaxing cruise disrupted this way.

"Yeah." It took Winston three steps to stand directly in front of her. She had to tilt her head back to look up at him. He reached up and with the back of his hand brushed away a few strands of hair that had come loose from the tightly twisted bun. That same hand traveled to her chin, preventing her from looking away from him. "And I plan to enjoy every minute of my spare time getting to know you."

The promise in his statement coupled with the look in his eyes made her go weak in the knees. She began to rock and blamed that on the ship moving away from shore.

"Winston," she whispered watching his mouth descend, "what are you doing?"

"Helping you keep the promise you made to me at the airport." He kissed her waiting mouth.

7

Maybe it was the alcohol. Possibly, the romantic atmosphere that floated around the deck like a love mist. Melanie wasn't sure what made her delay in pulling back. But she finally came to her senses.

"Don't do that!" she said, stepping back her hand shot to her mouth as if to protect her lips from another one of Winston's sensual assaults.

A dozen questions erupted in her mind, all struggling to push themselves to the forefront of her brain. She didn't appreciate the surprise appearance, or the weak explanation he just shared. But because she was so befuddled by how quickly she had reacted to his touch, she asked a question that she probably shouldn't have. It just popped out before she could stop it.

"Why do you kiss me the way you do?"

"How is that?" Winston asked, taking a step closer to her.

"Like you get so much joy out of it." He smiled and it dawned on Melanie that here she couldn't flirt and walk away as she had in the airport. At that time, she had figured she would never see him again. Now, she was trapped in the middle of the Pacific on a ship that was too small to hide on for long. And since Winston had not answered, not verbally anyway, she decided she should watch what she said from now on.

"I believe you can tell a lot about the way a person makes love to your body," he finally said, "by the way their tongue and lips make love to your mouth."

"I see." Melanie glanced around hoping no one had overheard that. She moved her hand away from her mouth, but since he was staring at it, she put it back.

Winston reached up and moved her fingers out of his way. His finger traced gently across her top lip. It stopped at her mouth's corner. Instinctively, she moved her lips across his finger. She caught herself doing that and stopped. Again she stepped back.

"That's exactly what I mean," he said. "I think making love to your body would be like dreaming when you're wide awake. If the way you kiss is any indication."

"Don't say such things to me," she managed softly.

"I answered your question," Winston explained.

"Just like you answered my other questions," she said. "In a way that suits your needs."

"What do you mean?" Winston, although sharp, was baffled.

"How could we be on the same ship and I not know about it?"

"I thought you would be glad to see me."

"You misled me, Winston. Why would I be glad about that?"

"I never said I wasn't going to be on this cruise."

"You never said you would be, either," Melanie responded defensively. She felt manipulated. "You could have told me when I mentioned it to you."

"You never gave me a chance, Melanie. You were too busy trying to get away."

"I did no such thing! You had ample opportunity."

"What difference does it make? I'm here now. And you want me to be."

"No, I do not!" She decided that she was angry. One hand went to her hip while the other pointed at him. "Don't you go manipulating the situation again."

"Didn't you say it would be a fantastic idea if I were on this cruise with you."

"I didn't mean it that way!"

"So you lied to me?"

"No!"

"Then you misled me?"

"Of course not!" She had been joking and now he was confusing the issue. "I didn't know you'd be here. I was kidding around."

"If *I* do it, it's manipulation. If *you* do it, it's kidding." He was flabbergasted.

"Yes...I mean, no!"

He just stared at her.

"Look," she said placing both hands on her hips. "It seems we're going to be trapped together for another seven days. I would appreciate it if you not approach me like you just did. Or the way you approached me on the plane for that matter."

"You told me you wanted more. I just gave you what you wanted."

She threw her hands up in the air before rubbing them across her hair. "I shouldn't be upset on my vacation. But I don't handle complications well," she said softly.

"I didn't think I was being complicated." He took a step toward her. "I'm not less than what you are expecting."

"Who said I was expecting anything?"

"Why else would you be upset?"

"Because I didn't expect you! It would be one thing if you walked up and just said hello. It's another to walk up and kiss me like you want more than that."

"What if I do?"

"I told you." Melanie forced herself not to shout at the man. "I'm not looking for a quick lay!"

"What about a good, slow lay?" he joked.

She laughed in spite of herself. Shaking her head, she said, "That's what I'm talking about. You can be so damn misleading. You knew what I meant, yet you twisted it to your own advantage."

"Winston!" Sandra's voice came out of the distance. She ran over to greet him. "Mel said you were in Papeete! A meeting or something."

"I was. The rest of the medical meetings will be aboard ship."

"Really?" Sandra said excitedly. "That means there's a boatload of doctors walking around loose." She looked around, hopeful. "Being able to do business and still mix in a lot of pleasure is great."

"That was the idea." He looked back at Melanie.

"You two keep talking," Sandra said. "Let me go find a drink. Hopefully with a single doctor attached to it! Be back." Off she went toward the crowd on the opposite side of the ship.

"She's glad to see me." Winston watched her leave.

"You didn't kiss *her*," Melanie said defensively.

"I think she would be even happier to see me if I did."

Well, he was absolutely right about that, Melanie thought. Sandra wouldn't stand here questioning a man about why he found her attractive enough to want to kiss her and dream about making love to her. She would be leading him to some place they could make it happen.

Instead, Melanie was being a stick in the mud. Why couldn't she be as free-spirited and accepting of pleasure as Sandra was? Well, because she didn't have casual affairs and she was damaged from her last relationship, was why. She was still allowing Ronald to live rent-free in her mind.

Thoughts of Ronald's deception and the resulting pain sprang up like a toilet leak, ruining any chance of her having a good time right now. She attempted to cap it, but the damage was done. She needed to get away and think. Think this through. Think about Winston and his strong desire for her. Think about how she was going to manage being trapped aboard this ship with him and not give in.

My Lord! This was supposed to be a peaceful vacation and a wonderful writing assignment. Looking out over the water, the slap slap of the ocean against the ship sounded like clapping. The faster the ship, moved the louder the clapping seemed. A crescendo of joy was moving below her. Behind her, people milled about merrily as the band started another island song. And beside her stood a man who made her insides sing.

All around her was a celebration of joy, yet she stood there brooding because she couldn't figure out how to take advantage of it. She wanted to stomp and scream at Winston for making her feel this way. But she knew the great feelings that he stirred weren't the reason for her lousy mood.

Forcing a smile, she turned to face him. "If we avoid each other, I'm sure this will be a great trip for the both of us because I can't play your word games. I've got a busy day tomorrow. I'm headed to bed. Excuse me."

"Melanie?" he reached for her arm.

She stepped out of reach and walked purposefully to the exit leading to the stairwell that would take her down several flights of stairs…away from Winston, away from her annoying thoughts, away from the merriment.

Then she would be in her room where she could think more clearly.

Yet, just then, she didn't know what she wanted to think about.

8

Cruise Day 1 – Raiatea Island

Melanie's notes on Raiatea: Raiatea means expansive sky. 10,000 inhabitants, only 75 sq. miles. Waterfalls cascading down mountain slopes. A fruit lover's paradise: pineapple farms, mango groves, banana trees, to name a few, are plentiful. A variety of Hibiscus flowers are in bloom all over the island.

"Go away!"

"Sandra, get up," Melanie pleaded. "We're in Raiatea. Let's go get breakfast, then visit the island."

"Why can't you just leave me here?" Sandra whined. "What time is it?"

"Eight."

"Good God, stop torturing me."

"It's your own fault. You shouldn't have been out so late."

"Don't blame me. It was the doctor, lawyer, and Indian chief's fault."

Melanie laughed. "What are you talking about?"

I met this doctor and his friend, the lawyer. We ended up going to the Cognac Social...for Cognac."

"Makes sense."

"About five Cognacs later, some joint's chief or Indian chief, I think, joined us. All I remember is making a joke about it. But hell," Sandra fluffed her pillow and crashed her head on it, "he could have been a chef from Indiana. I was so lit, I don't remember too much after saying hello to him."

"Sounds like you had fun." Melanie was adjusting her pale blue tank top into the sides of the matching shorts. Grabbing her straw hat, note pad, camera, tape recorder and bag, she headed for the door. "I'm going to grab breakfast then go research the island. Since there's no easy way to find each other, leave me a note here on where you'll be this afternoon and I'll try to find you."

"The next sound you hear will be my snoring."

"Sleep tight!" Melanie stepped out the door.

"Put the 'Do Not Disturb' on the door! I don't want the maid to wake me!"

"Okay."

One beauty of the smaller cruise ship was that eating could take place whenever and wherever a person wanted, with the exception of the exclusive restaurants on board, which required reservations. Melanie decided to reserve a place for dinner at *L'Etoile* then headed to *LeVeranda* for breakfast. She found a spot portside, so she could have a view of the island. The ship had not docked, but was anchored close to shore.

The sight of plush, foliage-covered mountain that ran the length of the island awed Melanie. Only a little over three thousand feet high, the mountain seemed to stretch to the heavens and appeared to be floating along the horizon as sky met ocean in an aqua blue, non-distinctive plain. It was named *Temehani'ura* and Melanie almost laughed out loud at the butcher job Sandra would do attempting to pronounce it. Inspired, she jotted notes about its beauty and feel.

"Good morning," a male voice said.

She looked up at the waiter. "Oh, hi!" Melanie snapped out of her reverie.

"Would you like a menu?"

"Tea, please, with cream. And I'll help myself at the breakfast bar."

"Certainly, Madam!" The server headed to the drink station.

Melanie went back to scribbling notes. As the tea was placed in front of her, she looked up to thank him, but couldn't get the words out.

"Winston?" she frowned.

"Good morning." He pulled out the chair next to her. "I was just about to head to my meeting but saw you here. May I join you for a minute?"

"I'm in the middle of...." Melanie stopped because he sat down.

"Of what?" He pushed her tea closer to her hand. "I had to wrestle this away from your server. I think he thought I wasn't going to give it to you. But you were saying?"

"Middle of the article I'm researching."

"You're a writer?"

"I freelance for magazines, journals, newspapers."

"I would love to read some of your work." Winston smiled, impressed. "I can't write anything more than a prescription."

"That's a talent within itself."

"I love your smile," he whispered, catching her off guard.

"Please, don't try...." Melanie began but Winston wouldn't let her finish.

"I know," he put a hand up to stop her. "Let me start by saying you were right last night. I did take advantage of the situation and I apologize for giving you the impression that I was manipulative in any way."

"You were."

"It's a small ship." He shook his head. "And I don't want to avoid you."

"If we do cross paths, I prefer you be more honest and direct with me."

"If I promise to speak as directly as possible and not hold back the truth, will you have dinner with me tonight?"

"Sandra and I have reservations," she said, hoping she could talk Sandra into joining her. She didn't know if she could handle his directness. The indirect approach was causing her to dream about him, pant for him, warm for him. She could possibly lose herself to him if he were to add open and honest to his modus operandi. And that scared her.

"Dr. Knight," a voice called from nearby and Winston turned to it. "You're needed."

"Thanks, Bob. I'll be there." Winston turned back to Melanie. "Then have lunch with me?" he said.

"I'm going to be on the island most of the day…researching."

"I have to do a presentation this morning. Else I'd blow off this meeting and tour with you. It should be over in an hour or two; maybe I could join you. Will leaving in the…" Winston mentally calculated the time. "…afternoon give you enough time to research?"

"Not really."

"Understood." Winston rapidly thought of other options. "When will you be back?"

"I don't know, Winston. Besides you need to go."

A thought hit him. "You know. When I think about it, I believe the issue with us was caused by timing," he said, nodding. "I only get snatches of time with you and I find myself saying things that will get me the response I want in the time I do have. But I promised not to manipulate the conversation like that again."

"Winston, you don't…."

"Dr. Knight?" It was Bob again. Winston gave him a quick nod then stood up as he reached to touch her hand.

"Let me hurry and say this so that it sounds right to you." He came around the table and squatted down in front of her. At almost eye level he said, "I like you, Melanie. And the fact that you've been on my mind since the moment I saw you is making me crazy, because this is very rare for me." He placed his hands on her thighs and squeezed. She looked down at them. "Touching you makes my fantasies all real." His whisper sounded like an ache. "You even tiptoed into my dream last night."

"Winston Knight," Chuck said, nearing the table. "I hate to break all this up, but we're on a tight schedule. You're needed now."

"Give me thirty seconds, Chuck."

"I was told not to come back without you." Chuck grinned at the murderous look his friend gave him. "So I can't leave, buddy."

"Then turn around and give me some privacy."

Winston leaned forward and kissed her quickly on the mouth. He whispered in her ear, "I'm hard and I haven't even seen the real you naked."

He stood and stared down into captivating eyes. Damn, he wanted to stay. "I hope that was direct enough for you."

Shocked, she managed to nod once. Maybe twice.

"Tell me a time to meet you onboard," he asked. "I want to finish this conversation."

"Uhm," Melanie was trying to take in all what was happening to her. After that brazen statement, she couldn't think of a suitable denial. "Around four."

"Where," he said as Chuck pulled at his arm.

She quickly looked at the cruise schedule hoping to find an event with lots of people to run interference, but nothing suitable was on the list.

"Any place, Melanie," Winston said.

"Here then." She would have to put parameters around how freely he entered her personal space and touched her body. "We do need to talk."

"This restaurant is closed at four," Chuck volunteered. "Quickly, Melanie, we have to go."

"Meet me at my stateroom," Winston decided. "Room 710."

"Okay," she agreed.

"Four o'clock. Room 710," Winston shouted before rushing out of the restaurant.

She should have told him off for saying what he did, but that didn't seem like the most appropriate response after being told she had been monopolizing his thoughts. And besides, she couldn't do it in the middle of a restaurant with his friend standing right there, she rationalized.

Who was she fooling? She enjoyed every second of knowing how she was affecting him physically. She had asked for directness and honesty, and she got it. That would teach her to be cautious about what she asked for.

Besides, she had dreamt about him too. She just didn't have the guts to tell him. Suddenly stimulated, she crossed her legs and felt wetness forming between them. Melanie reached for her cup as a slither of erotic joy raced down her spine, making her shudder. She dropped the cup. It clanked and rattled on the saucer.

"More tea, Madam?" The happy-to-serve waiter appeared with the kettle.

She needed more all right, but *tea* wasn't what came to mind. "No thanks." She refused to try to stand. She would give herself a few minutes before getting up to have breakfast.

Thirty minutes later, Melanie found the strength to leave the restaurant and head for the tender station to catch the motor boat to shore. She had decided on a guided tour that started in a safari vehicle with four other vacationers. They traveled through the mountain, which offered sweeping sea vistas. They stopped at *Marea Maputa-*

puatea, the largest sacred site in Polynesia. Its ancient stones made from volcanic rock were laid as sidewalks and were topped with larger stones that looked to Melanie is if they could have served as chairs and tables. It didn't hold much meaning for her until the tour guide detailed how this site was the temple of the sexually aggressive war god Oro around 1350 AD. She tuned in for more. It seemed sex was the only thing that got her full attention of late she thought with a grimace.

Melanie decided that pictures of the interior and lagoon would serve her memory better in describing this island in her article, so she settled on a canoe trip. But what started as a great idea turned problematic when a rain shower arose. The tour guide navigated the boat under large trees to protect them from the weather.

"We will wait here a few minutes," the guide stated with a thick Tahitian accent.

Melanie quickly glanced at her watch. It was two o'clock and this tour was scheduled to stop at the botanical garden.

I can still make it back in time, she thought.

One hour later, Melanie found herself pacing at the garden. How many damn pictures of flowers did these people need? She went to the tour guide, "Is it possible to hurry this along? I need to get back to the ship."

"No problem, Madam?" He went to point out the breadfruit trees that grew all over the island and began explaining how baking the fruit on an open flame resulted in a tasty treat that resembled bread. "Having food is no problem with this tree around," he explained with a grin. Then he proceeded deeper into the garden, not even pretending to pay heed to Melanie's request.

She hated it when people showed up late for dates with her; the least she could do was try to keep her appointment. And she was sure that the look on Winston's face and his reactions to her were proof that he would be on time. She found the guide again, "Is there a cab I can take?"

"No need, Madam. Besides, you may have to wait longer to get cab."

"I see," she glanced at her watch. She would definitely be late.

At five o'clock Melanie found herself racing onto the ship. She needed a shower after the wet, muggy experience on the island, but didn't want to delay any longer. She would go directly to his room first, make plans to meet him later, then go to her room to shower. Banging on the elevator button, her patience ran out before it came. She took the stairs from the tender station on Level 3 to Level 7. At his room, she knocked but got no answer. She waited in the hall for another ten minutes hoping he would return.

Tired of waiting she headed to the receptionist desk.

"Hello. If I need to find someone on the ship, what's the best way of doing so?" Melanie asked.

"I can call the room, Madam. Or you can leave a note that we can deliver for you," the so-called helpful woman said smiling.

"Please get this to Dr. Knight in room 710." Melanie scribbled a note, ending with asking him to call her. She passed it to the receptionist.

Melanie went to her room to shower and dress for dinner. Hopefully, he would call her in time to make the seven o'clock reservation. She called him a little after six and decided to look for him at poolside since a live-band event was taking place there. As she opened the door, Sandra strolled into the room.

"Heyyy, Girl!" Sandra said. "If I had known doctors could be this much fun, I would have dated a few at the hospital."

Melanie was hopeful. "Are they all meeting somewhere?"

"They were all at the restaurant next to pool. I saw Winston and Chuck there, too!"

"I'm headed up there to find Winston."

"Don't bother. They left right before I did. Everyone's going to take a quick shower and change for dinner. Most of them are planning to meet in the Casino Bar first."

"Winston, too?"

"He was already dressed and said he would meet us. But I wouldn't hang around him today if I were you."

Melanie turned around quickly, "Why? What did he say?"

"It was what he didn't say. That man's in a pissy mood."

Oh, no! It's all my fault. Melanie called him again. He didn't answer. "Sandra, I'm going up to see if Winston is in his room, else I'll meet you at the Casino Bar." She was out the door.

Melanie couldn't find him in his room, or poolside or the other places she checked. Entering the Casino Bar, she looked about. She saw Sandra at a table with two men, a few other faces she recognized but no Winston. Making her way through the rows of tables and mingling people, she joined Sandra.

"Hey, Girl!" Sandra said merrily. "Come sit here between Ralph and me. "Meet two of the threesome. Remember that Indian chief story? This is Dr. Marcus Lowell and Attorney Ralph Day."

Melanie greeted them before sitting. "So there was a real Indian chieftain?"

"No," Ralph, the lawyer, said. "He's a retired coach for the Kansas City Chiefs."

"Well, I was close!" Sandra retorted.

They all laughed.

"What are you drinking, Melanie?" Ralph asked. He leaned unnecessarily close to her.

"White wine."

"Let me go get you a drink."

Ralph returned, placed her drink on the table while touching her shoulder. He leaned over, "Anything else?"

"Breathing room," Melanie said.

Ralph found his seat. "So, Melanie," he said, "I hear you're a writer?"

Melanie turned to him after giving Sandra a don't-find-men-for-me look. "Articles not novels."

"Sandra said you were researching the romantic elements of French Polynesia. I can teach you a few things, starting with French kissing." Ralph placed his much-too-friendly hand on her shoulder and leaned toward her.

She was in no mood for this. As she was about to turn to tell Ralph to get his damn hand off her shoulder, she noticed Winston out the corner of her eye. "Excuse me," she said to the group, "I see a friend." She weaved through the crowd. When reaching the Casino Bar entrance, Winston was no longer around. She looked about before going outside into the corridor.

Nothing.

Hurriedly, she headed toward the nearest elevator. He wasn't waiting there either. Looking up the stairwell, she caught sight of the tail of his navy silk shirt.

"Winston!" she called, but the shirt kept moving. Now that angered her. Rushing up several flights of stairs she finally made it to the Level 7. She rounded the corner and saw him. "Winston, wait!"

He stopped but didn't turn around.

Out of wind from the stair climb, but fueled by anger, she approached him with an attitude. "I know you heard me calling you?"

He folded his arms across his chest as his eyes roamed slowly from her head, which was fashioned with her hair twisted in a loose bun with tendrils hanging, across her lovely face, to her ears adorned with ruby earrings, down arms covered with a long-sleeve sheer black blouse. He could clearly make out the details of the red lacy spaghetti strap blouse underneath. Her fitted black skirt went to the floor.

"So you weren't captured by natives," he finally said.

He was angry and she figured she deserved a little of this. "Did you get my note?"

"The one that came two hours late?"

"I didn't mean to be late." Melanie didn't want to have this discussion, but the excitement she had felt all day from knowing she would spend time with him made her keep going. Now realizing that it wasn't going to happen, she felt sapped. She would explain herself and leave. She didn't feel like arguing.

"Melanie, you asked me to be honest and direct with you. That's what I was this morning. I expected the same."

"I know. I didn't mean to be late. Everything went wrong near the end of my visit to Raiatea. It rained; that delayed the tour. Then I almost missed the last shuttle to the ship."

"I can accept that explanation," he looked briefly at her shoulder. "The part that confuses me is you and octopus man in the Casino Bar. I would have preferred you try to fulfill our date instead."

She had to think about that. "You mean Ralph?"

"Explain Ralph."

"I'm not sure if Ralph can explain Ralph. He's horny, possibly?" She laughed softly before shaking her head in disbelief. "I had met him about two minutes before seeing you. But I was there looking for you. I would have preferred you being next to me."

"Really?" He seemed surprised.

"Yes. But I see I've missed my date with you. I won't keep you." She turned and walked away. After about three steps, Melanie realized he wasn't going to stop her. And she refused to look back. She kept walking.

"Melanie?"

She turned slowly. He was still standing where she left him. Arms across chest, the side of him facing her with his head turned to look at her.

"Yes?"

"Did you wear that outfit for our date?"

She took two steps toward him. "My plan was to invite you to dine with me at *L'Etoile*. I would have worn this, yes."

He started walking toward her. "What else was in your plan for me?"

Until that very second Melanie couldn't read what was behind his stare. She had thought, until now, that he had written her off. But as he stopped in front of her, she could see the heat forming behind his stare. It was if she were thrown back in time to this morning. When he was telling her about his stiffness, telling her how much he wanted her, caressing her thigh, kissing her mouth.

"I also wanted to enjoy you," she whispered, finding it difficult to concentrate.

"Tell me how?" He turned her and pushed her back against the wall.

"By touch," she whispered, feeling his heat penetrating her clothing. He pressed her against the wall and pinned her there.

"You wanted me to touch you?" His hands were at her elbows moving tantalizingly up to her shoulders.

"Yes."

"I'm glad. I've thought about doing that all day." He stood back and admired the way the blouse enhanced her breasts. One hand undid several black buttons and found red lace underneath. "I like the way this feels." His hand was moving over the material covering her nipple. She wasn't wearing a bra, so he pulled the blouse away to expose all the red lace covering her breasts. He lightly caressed the tops of her breasts with his fingers.

"Me too," she whispered.

They were standing in a long, softly lit corridor. Mirrors and masterpieces covered the walls between doors to staterooms. They were very close to his room, but based on the way he looked at her, Melanie thought his desire would prevent him from making the short distance. He was going to have her right then and there.

Only the guests who lived on this wing would be in the area, and at this time of evening most were at dinner. But that didn't guarantee one of them wouldn't walk up on them in the middle of something stimulating. Melanie quickly glanced both ways. The hall was empty.

"Winston...." she managed as she felt him press his hardness between her legs. "We can't...not here."

"First, tell me where you wanted me to touch you."

Her mind attempted to form sentences but his mouth prevented her from speaking them. He kissed her. The kiss became fierce as he sucked her tongue, tasted her lips, licked her mouth.

In her ear he whispered, "Did you want me to nibble your ear?" He didn't wait for a response before doing so. "Did you want me to lick your lobe?" His tongue tasted the rim of her ear as she moaned.

"Yes."

"What about tasting your shoulder? Should I touch you there?" He was sucking and nibbling his way to her shoulder as he questioned her. "Shall I suck your tit?"

He bent to capture the hardening nipple through the soft material and she almost screamed.

"Hmmmm…ooohhhh, yesssss…" she managed. "Winston…."

Suddenly it ended, and Melanie slumped against the wall her senses clouded by the hot foreplay. Then awareness dawned; the sound she had heard and ignored was a door opening. Winston obviously was keenly aware of it, because he had already began righting her clothing. He pulled her by the wrist and marched her down the hall.

Melanie caught a glimpse of herself in a mirror and saw that her lipstick covered most of her lower face. She began correcting the damage.

"Dr. Knight?" a male voice called from behind.

Winston got a quick look at Melanie, then stepped in front of her. "Dr. Miller. Good evening. We were just heading to *L'Etoile* for dinner."

"Excellent! I was just headed that way myself." Dr. Miller had made his way down the hall and stopped near them.

Behind Winston's back Melanie had finished correcting the damage just as Miller arrived. She moved to his side. "Hello, Dr. Miller. I'm Melanie McDae."

"Hello. You're quite lovely. I know that name," Miller said. "I was reading something in *Travel Times*?"

"I have published several articles with them."

"I thought so! I might look like Father Time, but the mental faculties are still with me." He pointed to his temple. "I enjoyed that piece on Winter Wonderland." He smiled broadly, modeling an exquisite collection of caps, tooth implants and porcelain fillings. "Well, let's go to dinner! Besides, you two aren't doing anything else!"

9

What Winston really wanted was to explore Melanie's luscious body in private.

From the moment Dr. Miller appeared, he knew that wasn't going to happen. Winston had mentioned the dinner reservation as an excuse to get rid of Miller so he could take Melanie to his cabin to finish what they had started in the hall. He had already pulled his room key out of his pocket when Miller had called to him.

Once Miller made the dinner suggestion, Melanie reluctantly agreed. As they headed toward the restaurant, Winston began planning how he would invite her back to his room for a nightcap and hopefully the night.

But at the restaurant, Winston's dreams of privacy dwindled even more. As the headwaiter approached, Dr. Miller spoke out again. "They're dining with me and the renowned Dr. Michael Poole. Give their table to someone else and make room at my table!"

"*Oui…bien sur*," the headwaiter agreed in French.

"I would love to meet Dr. Poole," Melanie said to Miller. "I've heard a lot about his research in the Pacific."

Winston squelched the annoyance boiling inside. Because Dr. Miller was an elderly man who loved attention, he thought having dinner was the least he could do to help ease the pains aging had brought upon him. So Winston followed, laughing to himself at how his plans of seduction were squashed so quickly by a man twice his age.

L'Etoile had an elegant, romantic setting. Soft lighting with warm, cream colors and exotic plants. Windows covered three sides giving all a view of the moon kissing the ocean in glowing streaks. When they got to the large circular table in a corner near the restaurant's back windows, several people were seated. Winston shook hands with several of the men, introductions were made after everyone was seated and the waiter distributed menus. The wine steward arrived and took orders as they all sat making light conversation.

"Dr. Knight, " Dr. Poole said, "I understand you signed up for the scuba trip tomorrow."

Winston had met Poole briefly that morning when he had joined the doctors' meeting to brief them on the dolphin excursion. Poole, who resided in French Polynesia, was well known for the scientific research he had done on whales and dolphins for the past twenty years. He was also a special guest on the *Paul Gauguin*, lecturing on 'The Dolphin and Whale Population of the South Pacific' to all passengers interested.

"After hearing you speak this morning," Winston said, "I decided it could be quite interesting."

"The feeding habits and mating rituals of these mammals might not come in handy for what you do, but I guarantee it will be educational," Poole said.

"It sounds like it would be," Dr. Miller interjected. "But at seventy-three, I can't take that activity. I'll attend your seminar on board and leave scuba diving to the young bucks!"

"Mrs. Knight, you're more than welcome to join our dive trip if you're a certified diver," Poole offered.

Melanie was ordering wine and didn't realize the question was directed to her. She looked up and saw nine sets of eyes staring at her. Only Winston's held humor. When she reached for her water and gulped some, he decided to take pity on her and announce she wasn't married...yet.

Melanie answered before Winston could. "I'm going to be researching Tahaa tomorrow."

Winston looked down at her, surprised that she hadn't corrected Poole.

"Researching?" A doctor who looked to be in his early thirties asked.

"She's a writer!" Dr. Miller offered. "Did this great travel magazine piece on winter vacation spots in the highlands of Colorado. At my age, I wouldn't consider going to some place that reminds you of downhill skiing and high-speed snow mobiling. But her article talked about the relaxing, non-adventurous stuff like renting a cabin with an outdoor Jacuzzi. Heated walkways and warmers around it so you can sit in warm bliss in the middle of winter, ordering from restaurants that deliver, so you never have to leave. Those are the types of trips I like. Learned a lot about the history of Vail and Breckenridge as well."

"You're going to write about Tahaa?" the young doctor asked Melanie.

"I've been contracted by two women's magazine to do a kind of 'pampering Tahitian style' article. And I'll focus on Moorea and Bora Bora for that because those islands cater to people who can afford it. They're not as mainstream as Papeete, but are more sophisticated than Raiatea and Tahaa."

"A lot of rich people own places on Moorea and Bora Bora," Joy, a young doctor's wife, said. "That's if they don't go ahead and buy an island out here like Diana Ross and Marlon Brando did. I can see those two islands requiring spas and salons and things like that."

"Exactly," Melanie said. "Raiatea and Tahaa are more rural; mostly native farmers. I might include them as a place to obtain some of the great all-nature creams and health care remedies I've read about. I'm going to rent a bike and take my camera and see what I can see. I have the name of a bilingual guide who might help."

"Did you discover much on Raiatea?" Winston asked her.

"Lots. I'm thinking of renting a boat and traveling back there tomorrow, depending on what I find on Tahaa."

"Go back?" Miller questioned. "We left there at sunset and won't dock in Tahaa until nine tomorrow morning. Seems like a long ride back to me."

"The capital of Raiatea is only two miles, or a twenty-minute motorboat ride," another doctor offered. "These cruise ships just circle the islands or go out to sea and back to fill up your cruise time."

"I'll be!" Miller was amazed.

"I guess that's why they call it 'cruising,'" Winston said.

They all laughed.

As the dinner orders were being taken, Melanie moved her chair closer to Winston so the person on the other side of her couldn't overhear her. "Winston, why didn't you correct him? Now they all think we're married."

He placed his right hand in her lap. Her floor-length skirt was split on the side up to her thigh. Heat emanated from that split. He ran his fingers down the fronts of her thigh then back up the side nearest him. The thrilling shock waves ran up her naked leg then pooled between them.

"Do you really want me to disappoint these folks by letting them know I'm just a lonely, single man too weak to win the heart of a famous writer?"

"I'm..." she started and Winston enjoyed the way her tongue moistened her lips when she said that. "I'm not famous. Writing is just a passion," she whispered back.

He moved his mouth to her ear. "Do you have other passions?"

"I...uhm, teach." She looked around the table and he followed her gaze.

Everyone was chattering merrily, no one noticed that they had bowed out of the conversation. And from how Winston was positioned, it could have easily been interpreted as two people leaning close.

"Teach?" His hand squeezed her thigh and she looked back up at him. "Where?" His mouth came around to touch hers, exhaling warmth into her.

"Boulder University." Melanie leaned closer to him, placing her hand on his leg. "Are you changing the topic? You promised me directness."

"I haven't broken my promise to you. I didn't tell them that we were married. Nor did I hint at it. The question was directed to you."

"You should have said something."

"You brought this on yourself by not correcting them," Winston said. "Now, it's up to you to fix it."

"Me?" Her eyes held disagreement.

He leaned over and kissed her forehead. "Yes, you. Put your hand back. Don't stop touching me." He moved to press his lips to her ear. "Or I can tell them that I met you for the first time yesterday. Yet, it feels like much, much longer. And, that I'm so taken by you that I'm horny just thinking about how your nipple tasted when I kissed it." He leaned back to look into her eyes.

She was staring, wide-eyed, bewildered. "No, that's okay," she finally said, forgetting to whisper, "I'll handle it."

Winston placed one hand at the base of her neck and massaged that spot while his other hand found her hand that she has just placed back in her own lap.

"Melanie," he said. She looked up and he mouthed more than spoke because it was said so softly. "I want you to handle me instead." He needed to feel her on him. He placed her hand on his thigh then moved it up and down. Before turning his attention to the table, he said to her, "Please, keep it there."

"You need help handling something?" Dr. Miller interrupted from across the table.

"Melanie will handle it," Winston said.

"I'm sure she can handle anything she gets her hands on," Miller suggested.

"My thoughts exactly." Winston squeezed her hand. He fought back the need to grin at the look Melanie shot him. He knew full well that she had expected him to correct the misconception of marital status. And since he didn't, her look hardened. He suddenly feared she would jump up and shout the truth, embarrassing everyone. He needed a distraction to forestall her.

"Would you like to order, Madam?" the waiter said and Melanie almost jumped in surprise. Her hand left Winston's lap.

"*Oui,*" Winston agreed in French.

Because Winston responded in French, the waiter switched languages and continued in French. When Melanie looked up, clueless, Winston took over the conversation. This will distract her, he thought.

He picked up the menu, held it in front of Melanie, pointing out the meals written on the menu in English. Melanie nodded when his finger landed on dishes she wanted. He would quickly switch back to English to confirm what she wanted before continuing in French.

"Is that all you want?" he asked. She nodded and the waiter moved away. When Melanie placed her hand back in his lap, he said, "I like your touch." He never took his eyes off the wine list. Now that he had decided on his meal he wanted to order wine. He looked up and got the attention of the wine steward. "Would you like anything else to drink?"

"A refill, thanks," she said. "Are you always this attentive?"

"I call it making sure you're having a good time," Winston said.

"Do women always have a good time with you?"

He looked at her for several long seconds before answering. Something in her eyes said his response to that question was critical. "I'm only interested in whether you enjoy me."

"I do." She looked away. "Probably more than I should."

After dinner, Melanie and Winston took a stroll along the top level. Another couple was in the area at the front of the ship with them, but soon left. They were topside, alone.

Stopping to look out over the water, Melanie said, "How serene. These islands are incredible."

"I get the feeling this place is more like a quietness that should be enjoyed."

Melanie started laughing.

"What?" he asked.

"Well, what do you think serene is, silly man?" She giggled again.

"I'm a master at keeping calm," he said, and she noticed he wasn't smiling. "I would think serene would include some form of happiness combined with calmness."

His answer stopped her laughter. She wanted to know what had caused him to become so serious. "Does it have to include joy for you?"

He placed his hands on the guardrails and looked out into the darkness. "I get snatches of enjoyment, here and there. I haven't figured out how to put my work aside so that I can have longer periods of it. Serene is something that is out there." His hands went out as if including anywhere but near him. "I have a demanding career that dictates that I'm always on top of it. Even when I'm not working. I'm not sure if that represents happiness. I know damn well it doesn't represent serene. This is a perfect example. I'm cruising a place people dream of being and I've been working since I got here."

"Do you want to enjoy this trip more?" she asked.

He looked into understanding eyes. "I get the feeling you are an expert at it. Like your tomorrow. Renting a bike to see what you can see. Taking pictures. Hanging out with natives. You'll end up laughing, enjoying the day. I'll be studying sea life and lecturing on preventive health care."

Hearing the frustration in his voice, she moved closer. "You can come with me, if you like."

"I would love to, but I've got this thing…this presentation I'm expected to do." Before Melanie found a response, he continued. "I envy you. You write because it's your passion. You love doing it. But I entered medicine because I was expected to follow in my father's footsteps. I stay in it because it's what I do. Luckily for me, I'm good at it."

"Are you sure you haven't forgotten a few things that were fun in your life?" she cajoled. "I heard you speak French. I only know a spattering of it, but I got the impression yours was learned through interaction. Like you lived some place it was spoken."

He laughed, but it held no humor. "Melanie, I'm telling you this because you asked me to be direct with you." He exhaled and looked directly into her eyes. "At eighteen, right after I graduated, I was put on a plane with four hundred dollars, some books about France and a reference book on how to live cheaply abroad. My father had worked there before, so I had a visa to live there. I told him I wanted to return to France for a while instead of going to medical school. To teach me a lesson, he dumped me there and told me to survive. He had a friend there whom I could contact if I got desperate." Winston looked down at the water crashing against the ship. "Calling his friend would have meant that I had failed. I refused to fail. I learned the language in order to eat, to live, to keep from being abused in that country."

Melanie could not contain her shock and was grateful that Winston was still looking at the sea. Or else he would have seen her disapproving frown. "How did you survive?"

"One day, when I know you very well, I'll tell you the dirty details. But well after all the money was gone and food consisted of visiting restaurant dumpsters, I found an old woman with a warm spirit and a sickly body. I took care of her: cooked, cleaned, ran errands, repaired her home. Did the things she couldn't do for herself. In return, she gave me shelter and a little money. My father didn't think I would last six months. I stayed two years."

Melanie's heart felt as though someone had just hit it with a hammer. She inhaled deeply, trying to keep her body from tensing. America's streets were filled with starving teenagers who were abused and dying because of parents who had put them out. How could someone be expected to survive those conditions with the added burden of being in a strange, foreign place? It seemed to Melanie that Winston was caught up in being what everyone—except himself-wanted him to be. She wondered if he were given a chance to live his life over again, whether he would do things differently. The probable struggles he must have endured bounced around in her brain. How long had he gone without love?

Yet, somehow Winston was balanced and strong and loving. He must have been exposed to a caring environment at some point to allow him to have such a strong spirit. What he had become was a man driven to be better than was expected. And that was a great characteristic.

Concerned because she brought up the topic of his past, she felt the need to help mend. Melanie stepped close to him and massaged his back with one hand as the other went around his chest. If touching was what helped him feel better, she would do it. She laid her head against his shoulder as she hugged him. She wanted to reach out and grab a piece of the serenity that surrounded them and wrap it around him.

"Winston?"

"Yes?"

"Dance with me?" She looked up into his eyes.

"I think there's a band at the Connoisseur Club."

She took his arm and pulled him away from the rail. "Dance with me here."

"Here?" He looked slightly confused, slightly eager. "Don't we need music?"

She stepped into his arms. "The sound of the wind and the ocean will be our music. But I can sing if you like?"

"Do you know any great oldies?"

She looked out into the quiet blackness of the still night. Stars sprinkled the heavens and the moon kissed a path across the calm sea. A cool breeze swept the deck. It smelled of peace and joy and goodness—the way wonderful days ended in places like this.

A song came to mind and she smiled. "I sure do." Melanie began humming Louis Armstrong's *What a Wonderful World*. Her humming may not have been the best, but once they started moving with rhythm she stopped. Alone, on the deck of the ship with the moon as their spotlight, they danced. She held him close as the music of the waves picked up where she had left off.

Ten minutes later the dancing had stopped, but they stood holding each other very close. Finally, Winston stepped back, and she saw him smile.

Thankfully, he was smiling again.

He took her hand and led her inside and down the hall to the elevator. Once inside, he pressed the number to her deck level.

When the doors opened, Melanie wasn't sure if she wanted to go back to her room. She looked down at her watch. It was one in the morning. Neither had spoken since the dance. She wanted to break the silence and somehow extend her time with him. Things were going so right now.

Now, as they stepped out of the elevator, he said, "You have a good day tomorrow and get some rest." Those words told Melanie the evening was indeed over.

"Okay." They stopped outside her room door. "Thank you, Winston, for inviting me to dinner."

He smiled. "I distinctly remember that you invited me to dinner."

"Oh, that's right!" Her laugh was catching. "I did."

"I've never enjoyed dinner more," he said, the sparkle returning to his eyes. He kissed her on the forehead as he hugged her close. "Good night." He turned to leave.

She watched him take several steps.

"Winston?"

He turned, over ten feet way, to looked at her.

She took a single step. "Thanks for the dance too."

"Any time."

She stood watching as he walked away. He never looked back and she wondered if it had to do with the hint of melancholy in his eyes when she mentioned the dance.

10

Cruise Day 2 – Tahaa Island and Motu Mahana

Melanie's notes on Tahaa: Tahaa is even quieter than Raiatea. Only 4,470 inhabitants, who either farm, fish or raise livestock. Famous black pearls aplenty. Called Vanilla Island because of abundance of vanilla bean farms, their black gold. Crime is unheard of here.

"Sandra, I'm going to rent a bike and ride around Tahaa," Melanie said placing her camera, tape recorder and notepad in her backpack. "It's only about 42 miles of road. Sure you don't want to come?"

"That sounds like work, not play." Sandra was tying a *pareu*, the popular Polynesian oversized cotton scarf, around her waist and it hung to the floor. "I'm going to the Motu Mahana. Snorkeling, kayaking and lying in the shade is the most I'm going to do today. I think it's the ships private motu. I'll have lunch there, too, since they're barbecuing."

"Speaking of food," Melanie said, "make reservations at *LeGrill* for tonight before you leave. I'll be starving when I get back."

Melanie took the stairs down to Level 3 to catch the tender service to the island. Black pearl farms were unique to French Polynesia. She wanted to spend time at the cultured pearl farms to not only discover how the pearls were raised and harvested but also to buy some for herself and her mother. Her mother, Candice McDae, always stressed that Black is beautiful. Melanie knew this would be the perfect gift. Black pearls, despite the name, developed natural colors that ranged from misty black to pearly white. Melanie was intrigued by the array of colors found on this farm, which included deep olive green, bluish-purple, pink and champagne. Since the pearl farms didn't have the ridiculous markup that the shops would, she purchased three golden-hued pearls to have set in a necklace with diamonds and the precious golden stone, citron. She also brought one large misty black pearl to have made into a ring for her mother.

That accomplished, she headed out by bike to find the guide who was to assist her in her visits to other farms and villages.

Five hours later, Melanie was complaining to herself that a bike tour up, down and around hilly roads was an absolute nightmare. She returned to the ship walking like a woman sixty years her senior. A long, hot soak in the Jacuzzi would do the trick, but first she would take a shower, rub down in Ben-Gay, and then take a nap.

"Mel!" Sandra's shouting woke Melanie from her nap. "Oh, did I wake you up?"

"No," Melanie sat up and stretched. "I had to get up to see what all the yelling was about."

Sandra laughed. "Well, I'm back!" Was her only explanation. "I made dinner reservations for seven. I'm going to take a shower then head up to the piano bar. Take in some music and sip some wine. Wanna come?"

"You have fun." Melanie got up and moaned from the soreness in her legs. "I'm going to the spa. First Jacuzzi, then steam room. I should get back in time to change for dinner."

Whatever aches and pains Melanie had when entering the Carita Spa had eased considerably as she stepped out of the Jacuzzi. She put on a robe and went to the therapy room she had reserved. Each room had a vanity area filled with body care items and towels, a separate shower stall and enclosed steam room. She disrobed, picked up the body gel and shampoo off the vanity and headed to the shower stall.

Smelling like vanilla and feeling quite refreshed, Melanie stepped out of the oversized shower stall and went to the steam room. Opening its glass door, she could barely make out the design of the room at first until the gush of steam billowed out and subsided. The hissing steam came from a heating unit in the middle of the room. Dim lights reflected on the long benches along the walls. Heading to the wide bench to her left, she laid several towels over the bench before stretching out atop them.

Exhaling contentment she reflected on the trip's success so far: The tropical islands were wonderful; Sandra was enjoying herself; the weather was always pleasant; and her research today was enlightening.

Then she thought about the one thing that had not gone as planned: Winston. What had happened last night, she wondered? Something had brought a change to his personality. Once past their heated discussion over being so late, making up was delightful.

But the dance?

Melanie suggested it as a means to somehow share with him the possibility of what serenity meant to her. During the dance, he held her close and whispered things in French in her ear. It sounded like music to her, and the way he touched her while he spoke, made her think the words were erotic, provocative in nature.

Maybe I should ask him to translate what he said to me.

Then Melanie thought about their dinner conversation and the heated words he had said during it. *Maybe I won't.* That could be dangerous to her resolve, and she was already unable to turn away from him. This was strange to her because emotional relationships had not been a priority in a long time. Certainly, she had gone on dates. But it never got past the friendship stage with her. Too much pain and damage from Ronald's jealous and abusive ways, possibly. Instead, for the last year, she had concentrated on healing her broken spirit, advancing her career, enjoying time with her parents and bonding more with close friends like Sandra. Since just after college, Sandra had been living several states away, but they had agreed to spend time every year traveling to some exotic place. Ronald had never agreed to let that happen, so the trips didn't start until after the breakup. Melanie was content now with how the rest of her life had been going since she took control of it again; everything was going as planned.

Then Dr. Winston Knight invaded her thoughts, much like the way he had invaded her life. From the moment she had seen him it had been that way. In the airport jewelry store, she found herself locked in a trance that she couldn't, or didn't want to break free from. Something about it made her warm and cool all at once. When he kissed her and it felt like nothing familiar yet very familiar all at the same time. She couldn't explain it, but something about the way his mouth explored hers was as if he had known it by memory and had at long last found it again. It also seemed like he pulled a little of her from it and stored it, in safety, inside of him. And with every kiss that followed he gave her a chance to visit and reunite with the parts of her that he held stored. She could bond with, be with, fully enjoy all of him and all of herself as long as his lips touched her.

And the way he appeared in person whenever she thought about him also made her wonder.

Just then the steam seemed to clear the room again, as if the door had been opened. Since she was lying on her back, facing away from the door, she tilted her head back to see.

"Oh, God!" she jumped up noticing a man walking into the shower stall. She sat up straight, placing her hands over her exposed breast.

"I didn't mean to scare you," Winston said.

"Winston?" She was completely nude and the closest towel was under her butt or across the room. Reaching for either would result in exposing more of her body. And since he was standing in front of her with only a towel around his waist, displaying a completely magnificent physique, she kept completely still. Looking up at him she said, "What are you doing in here?"

"Disturbing your relaxation." Winston retrieved the towel and gave it to her. "You can lie back down now."

She ignored that as she adjusted the towel over the front of her. "How did you get in here? This is my private room."

"Funny story really," he said sitting next to her. "Sandra told me you were here. I thought to join you in the Jacuzzi. As I had walked into the lobby of the spa, Dr. Miller was about to leave. He had just finished his massage. He asked about my wife and the receptionist told us you were in the steam room. Then she asked, since I was your husband and all, if I wanted to join you. I told her that was an excellent idea. I showered and here I am."

Melanie's bottom jaw moved up and down as if attempting to speak words, but nothing came out. Finally she formed a few, "Winston, you've got to let the people on this ship know that we're not married."

"Uh, huh," he grunted noncommittally. He changed the topic. "Lie down, finish steaming."

"This is a bit too forward. Why come in here?"

"I needed to apologize for something."

"You can start with for coming in here," she suggested. "Couldn't everything else have waited 'til I finished steaming?" she said in disbelief.

"It wasn't my idea to join you in here, I came for the Jacuzzi remember? Besides this is a big room, large enough for a dozen people. Why don't you share it with me? The steam would do me good after that full day with the dolphins. It felt more like work than play."

"Since you seem to think your logic clears all this up," she said surprised she didn't mind his invasion, "Let's move on to the reason you came. What did you want to apologize for?"

"I realized something last night." He looked down at her. The steam softened her already tranquil features. "That maybe my approach to you was a bit strong."

Melanie found herself laughing. It was a musical sound that filled the room. *It was very strong, incredibly demanding and downright sensual* were Melanie's thoughts, but she didn't voice any of it because he was talking.

Winston leaned back, placing the back of his head against the wall. His shoulder was touching hers. Reaching over, he placed his hand on her bare thigh and squeezed. Exhaling gruffly he said, "I came after you like I approach everything I've ever wanted. But that's not fair because I didn't give you a chance to decide if you wanted this...or to have anything to do with me." Winston turned his head to look down at her again, "I guess I wanted to apologize for that."

"Is that it?" Melanie asked thinking to accept his apology if he was finished with his explanation.

"No," he offered. "I also noticed you're a pretty good dancer to the sound of nothing."

"We danced to the wind and ocean noises, remember."

"And it was the dance that made me think I should slow down with you. Let you decide how we should spend our time together. I enjoyed the dance and would hate to think that I might not get to do that again."

He sounded so tender and vulnerable to her. She wanted to hug him for the heartfelt statement. Obviously her feelings were important to him. "Don't worry about it," Melanie said. "To be honest, your approach was a bit surprising and unsettling. And I swear I don't know how to handle you."

"Then, why do you?" he asked softly.

"Promise not to laugh?" she asked and he nodded. "Back in the airport, I had looked across the counter at you and something in your expression touched me. In a good way."

"Like love at first sight?" he asked smiling. He turned his body to her. His knee was touching her thigh as he caressed it.

"I don't know if I'd say that," she smiled. "I just know that you're not the first man who has approached me aggressively. You're just the first that I've let go so far."

"Why?"

Her response didn't require any second thought. "I like you," she said softly.

"I'm glad you said that," Winston lifted the corner the towel that covered her body. He used it to wipe away the wetness on her face and neck. Melanie never took her eyes off his, nor did she try to cover her exposed chest. "I'm *very* glad you said that." He pushed her body back so she was lying on the towels again, her legs behind him as he turned toward her. With the towel, he rubbed down her arms, over her full breasts, along her sides, across her flat tummy, then down one thigh. Standing, he lifted one of her legs, so it was bent as he rubbed the fresh steamy wetness from around her legs.

"Relax, Melanie," he whispered seductively. "Nothing that you don't want to happen will." He used the towel to remove the buildup of fresh steam from his body before folding it and placing on the floor in front of him. Then he knelt on it. "I need to feel you, Melanie. May I?"

She couldn't see the details of his expression, but clearly he seemed to be taken by the sight of her nudeness and indulged himself. That warmed her insides as much as the room did the outsides. "It's too soon for intercourse."

"I'm just asking to explore you all over," he said.

"I don't understand."

"If you don't want intercourse, just let me touch you the way you want to be touched."

She wasn't quite sure what that meant, but it sounded so appealing that she couldn't refuse. She reached for his hand and placed it between her breasts.

As his hand traveled down the front of her body, his mouth came down on hers. She wrapped one arm around his neck and pulled him down for more. His mouth opened over hers again and again as the kiss intensified. Tongues tangoed as lips sought and found more pleasure.

"I love the taste of you," he said as his hand caressed her breast. "All of you." His mouth moved to her neck as he licked a wetter path to the breast he held. As his fingers fondled its fullness, his mouth lovingly assaulted one taut nipple.

Melanie lifted slightly moving her breast deeper into his hungry mouth. He licked the underside of her arm, then nibbled down the skin covering her ribs. Melanie turned toward his mouth bending a knee as his mouth found her hard, extended nipple again. "Yes... Win..." she moaned as the excitement roared through her body. He placed his hand between her parted legs and massaged back and forth, back and forth. "Oh, God!" She called, opening her legs wider.

He kissed downward, down past her ribs, past her navel and over and down to silky hairs. She let out a scream when his mouth replaced his hand between her legs. The more he tasted the more she needed to be tasted.

"Winn......ston..." she called as his finger pressed inside her while his mouth found her pleasure spot. The sensations overwhelmed her, shook her. A strange, delicious wave of an incredible feeling took hold, scintillating her. She trembled as tiny electric sparks burst within her. Running everywhere, starting from where Winston's mouth touched her and splattered to her head, her toes.

She reached for Winston. "Winston! I...can't..." she panted. His mouth moved away from her body. "...breathe. What..." The shock wave hit her again. "I feel...." She felt a hand against her forehead, then neck, both hands on her arms.

"I have you," he said, lifting her off the bench. "It must be the heat in this room. Baby, don't worry...."

She closed her eyes and felt herself floating away. Whatever was happening to her lessened but never entirely stopped. It made her tremble. Then she felt coolness, soon followed by a cold hardness against her back. She was standing.

"I'm going to turn on the shower," she heard him say.

Melanie finally opened her eyes and realized she was in the shower stall. Lukewarm water went down her back as Winston's hot body pressed her against the back wall. His knee pressing between her legs helped her stand.

"It's okay now," he whispered and kissed her cheek.

She moved her mouth to press her lips to his. She inhaled the air he breathed then wrapped her arms around his neck. The powerful sensation that had started in her body earlier began to bubble inside again as Winston's thigh pressed between her legs. The excitement called to her. She moved her hips, rubbing her womanhood against his manhood.

He leaned back. "Melanie?" he asked, but her open mouth found his again.

She pulled him closer. "Touch me like that, again," she whispered moving her body against his leg. "Yes," she said when his hand found the hidden spot between her legs. "Like that...yes." She began grinding his hand. "I need...I don't..."

"Let me make this better," he said.

"Pleeeeassse...."

The towel around his waist dropped. He lifted her and she wrapped her legs around him. Then he shoved the length of his fullness inside her, gyrating before one more thrust.

She moaned in pleasure. "That's it...." she managed to say.

He thrust again, then again and her body began to shake and tremble. Her moans ricocheted around the room. She went limp against him, heart racing, her breathing hard.

Minutes later, Winston turned off the water. She put her legs down as he held her close. She had her arms around him, her face against his chest, her eyes were still closed.

"Melanie?" he whispered against her ear. "Baby, can you stand?" She nodded and did so. "Look at me."

A few moments later she did. Thinking how incredible the experience was, she said silently, "What just happened to me?" Not until Winston responded, had she realized she had spoken aloud.

Leaning forward, he kissed her brow, then nose, then mouth. "Sounds to me like you had an orgasm. Possibly two," he whispered, reaching around her to pull her closer.

11

"Mel! Are you in here?" Sandra called entering the cabin. "Melanie?" she called again.

Melanie was standing on the other side of the room, looking out at the sea. With her back still to her friend, she said, "Am I the most pitiful excuse for a woman that you've ever seen?"

Sandra came to stand next to her. "What are you talking about?"

"What did I ever see in Ronald?" Melanie asked the glass. "How could I get to be twenty-eight-years-old and not understand orgasms?"

Sandra reached out and pulled Melanie around to face her. "Why don't I understand what you're talking about?"

"I don't understand either." Melanie needed to talk and with Sandra being the self-proclaimed sex expert, Melanie figured she was the best one to talk to. "That's my point."

"Let's back up a minute so that I can catch up," Sandra said. "Because I want to participate in any conversation that deals with orgasms."

Melanie grinned, shaking her head at Sandra's boldness. She wished she had been so free about the subject. It might have come in handy earlier.

"Last thing I knew about Ronald was that you were married to him for almost five years. But you divorced him a year ago even though it took the asshole some time to figure that you would. But you haven't heard from him in a while. I got that part. Now, what's with the misplaced orgasm?"

"I had one today!"

"Thinking of Ronald?" Sandra made a face, "Yuck!"

"With Winston."

"You kinky bitch!" Sandra joked. "What, you masturbated while thinking of him?"

"No, *with* Winston. He was there all right." Melanie went and sat on her bed, leaning back against the headboard.

Sandra hooped and hollered! "Thank you, Jesus! It's about time! Over a year is a *llooonnnggg* time to go without any. We should be celebrating, not moping!"

"I can't," Melanie said miserably. "I'm embarrassed over what happened."

"Look, embarrassed and orgasm can't go in the same sentence together. If you're beating up on yourself because you slept with Winston in record time, then don't. This man is serious about you. And you know I can tell that kind of thing."

"It's not Winston that's got me upset, but how inexperienced I am. I never had an orgasm before. I was taken so much by it I stood blabbering about how I didn't know what had happened. All this time, I thought that bullshit I was doing with Ronald was love making. I'm clueless."

"You're kidding, right?" Sandra said in disbelief. "Wait. Let me sit for this." She found a seat on her own bed.

"I was a virgin when I married him. Saving myself, I thought, for my husband to teach me how to make love." Melanie shook her head. "The wedding night was awful. And it didn't get much better after that. Then he injured his knee and his football career went up in smoke. With him being drunk most of the time made sex downright disgusting. I was relieved when he started cheating on me. I figured it was better for him to screw someone else, then me going through it. He even resented me for reaching my goals. Blamed me for everything, even *his* failures."

Sandra leaned over, resting her elbows on her knees. "I'm your best friend. And I'm totally amazed at hearing this."

"Nobody wants to flaunt pain and embarrassment. People tend to hide that even from friends."

"That ain't right," Sandra said. "Girl, you're about to make me cry."

"Don't. Else I'll start crying too. I knew something was wrong with our sex life. One night I asked him to do things to make it better. He told me he never had problems with satisfying women in bed before. I was the problem."

"And today you found out differently with Winston," Sandra said merrily.

"In addition to making me miserable, the thoughtless SOB didn't even give me an orgasm. How pitiful of a life is that?" She laughed, but it held no joy.

"Was it that good with Winston?"

"Sandra…It was…." Melanie thought back on it. She tingled from the memory. Smiling, her voice dreamy, she said, "I don't even know how to describe it. It was incredible. I couldn't catch my breath. It shook me to the bone. I felt like I was floating and dreaming and flying and having chocolate all at the same time!"

They both laughed.

"It felt so good!" Melanie added. "I felt it all over me…and it seemed to go on forever. And when I thought it was over, it started all over again."

Sandra's mouth dropped open. She was stunned—a rarity-into silence. She reached for her purse and pulled out her cigarettes. Alcohol and good sex always required one. She lit one up. "Wait a minute." She took another long drag. "I want to make sure I got this right." She stood and paced a few seconds. "Sounds like multiples. You mean to tell me…that your first time out," Sandra pointed the cigarette at Melanie, "you had multiple orgasms? Were you two at it all day? I thought you went for a bike ride…I should have figured when you were asleep…."

Melanie cut her off. "It was less than a half-hour. And after I got back."

"What?" Sandra shouted before saying, "All I want to know is does the man have a twin brother!"

"Sandra, be serious for a moment."

"I am," she took another drag off the cigarette. "As a heart attack."

"I'm too embarrassed to see him again. He probably thinks I'm some clueless, inexperienced…." Melanie stopped because Sandra was choking on the smoke she had swallowed by accident.

"Don't want to see him again?" Sandra yelled. "Have you lost your mind!"

"Sandra, I didn't know what was happening at first," Melanie said her voice full of shame. "Then when it was over I admitted I didn't know. He was probably feeling sorry for me and damn proud of himself when he told me I had an orgasm!"

"I can see your dilemma. I tell you what," Sandra said matter-of-factly. "This flying and floating stuff you're talking about is news to me. And I thought I knew it all. If you're not going to sleep with the man anymore, I am." Sandra was laughing as she resumed pacing.

"Sandra, please be serious!" Melanie started to laugh in spite of herself. She knew her friend would never sleep with a man she had expressed an interest in.

"Look." Sandra stopped and pointed her cigarette at Melanie. "It's against my religion to let an orgasm-making machine go unattended. One of us *GOT* to do it! I prefer it be you!" The cigarette was back to pointing. "Since you like the man and all. But I'll take up the slack if need be."

Melanie got up. She could always talk to Sandra about anything. Now that she was doing so, her misery was lessening. "I've moped about this long enough. Let me go throw water on my face so we can head to dinner. Besides, talking to you is getting ridiculous anyway."

Sandra turned serious. "Ronald was an old sore for you. Them tears you're crying inside right now are the pus from it. That sore can heal now."

"Sandra," Melanie said over her shoulder. "Stay away from philosophy. That pus analogy is turning my empty stomach."

"Stop complaining," Sandra whined, "You feel better don'tcha?"

"Yes. But I still haven't decided what I'm going to do about Winston. I just can't see the man again. And I'm stuck on this ship!"

"Let's talk about that—and the techniques he used on you-over dinner. I need to take notes on this floating thing."

"I'm not giving you the details!" Melanie said. "I've already confided too much."

"There's more you're not telling?" Sandra sounded hurt. "Just because I never told you details doesn't mean...."

The phone rang.

"Don't answer it!" Melanie screamed from the bathroom. "It will be Winston. And I'm not sure if I have the courage to talk to him right now," Melanie said coming out of the bathroom.

The phone rang again and Melanie and Sandra looked at it.

"Don't....!" Melanie's scream stopped short when Sandra picked up the telephone.

"Sandra's and Melanie's room!" Sandra said in a sing-songy voice. "Winston? What a surprise." She looked at Melanie then arched her eyebrows.

Melanie mouthed the words: Tell-him-I'm-not-here.

"You want to speak to Mel?" Sandra watched Melanie shake her head *'no!'* "She's in the bathroom right now."

"You want to hold?" Sandra said slowly.

Melanie mouthed the words: I'm-in-the-shower.

"She's using the toilet," Sandra said and shrugged when Melanie balled her fist at her.

"You're thinking of coming to the room, Winston?"

No! Melanie mouthed, shaking her head.

"Well..." Sandra's creative juices started to flow, "I'm not sure if that's a good idea." Sandra took the last puff of her cigarette then crushed it in the ashtray. "You see, Melanie was a little under the weather when I got here. No, not sick. But something happened today. She wouldn't tell me the details, mind you, but I think she wants to think it through. I think I'll take her to dinner so we can have some gal-bonding time. Make her feel better."

"No..." Sandra said to Winston's question, and Melanie wondered what they were talking about. Melanie came to stand in front of her.

"Melanie didn't say anything about you being the cause. But if this is your fault, then I think you should come up with something damn romantic to do to fix it."

Sandra laughed after listening for a few seconds.

"The phrase is: something *damn* romantic. Damn is a required word." He must have repeated it because Sandra said, "Those three words coming from a man is like music to my ears! Of course my favorite three words are 'here's my checkbook.' But that's another matter..." Sandra turned, bending to hang up. "Okay...I'll tell her. Bye."

"What all did he say?" Melanie asked.

"You heard." Sandra walked around her heading to the closet to get a change of clothes. "In the future, don't be getting me the middle of your sex life with him again, unless, of course, you have videos."

Melanie laughed at that.

"He didn't say it, but I think he knew you were listening in. Winston knows you're in hiding."

"If you hadn't answered the phone, he would *not* have!" Melanie corrected.

"Not answer?" Sandra feigned shock. "And miss the goofy expressions you were making trying to talk without making a sound? Never!"

Thirty minutes later Melanie and Sandra were in *LeGrill* having dinner. Sandra was starved and was enjoying her perfectly seasoned steak while Melanie, too flustered to eat, picked at hers.

"It's not a crime, Mel."

"Speaking of crime," Melanie changed the topic. "Did you know that on these smaller islands it practically doesn't exist?"

"No, I didn't." Sandra picked up her glass of wine and stared at Melanie before adding, "But I was saying that sleeping with Winston isn't a crime and you know it."

"Yes," Melanie said. "And I don't think you're going to drop the matter."

"Correct," Sandra agreed. "So what happened?"

"Let's just say Winston is a master of manipulation." Melanie was thinking of how Winston had let the husband assumption get him into her private room in the spa. "And every time he does it, I end up being overwhelmed by him."

"When I was with Winston earlier," Sandra said, "he wanted to invite you for drinks before dinner. I told him you were in the spa. So I'm assuming he stopped by the spa or ran into you before you got there."

"He met me at the spa," Melanie admitted. "Steam room to be exact."

"And that's when things got hotter!" Sandra said. "I'm always naked when I'm in one. Lord, you gotta love the man's approach!"

"With him in there with just a towel on, makes it hard to think straight."

"Thinking is the least of my concerns when I'm with a man that good looking who's practically naked," Sandra admitted. "But you're stressing over this. I know you're not going to give me details, but give me enough to figure out what went wrong."

"Winston knows how bad I am at it," Melanie admitted grimly. "I was so turned on I said things I shouldn't have. Damn near fainted."

"If you enjoyed him and he knows it then that's a good thing," Sandra said. "Just because you said something to the contrary ain't all bad. In the throes of passion, people say all kinds of things."

"What's bothering me more than anything else is how right Ronald was. I can't please a man."

"You've got to turn loose of that misery, Mel," Sandra said solemnly. "Forget about your past."

"I wish it was that easy," Melanie picked at a piece of meat. She couldn't look at Sandra either when she said, "When it was over today, I knew Winston hadn't ejaculated. I'm having orgasms all over the place and he didn't have any. I was so disappointed with myself that I had walked away."

"You're being too hard on yourself," Sandra said. "The best way to figure out how to please a man is to ask him. I hate it when a man tries to make love to me the way he did his last lover. What you should be doing is figuring out what Winston likes and not worry about what Ronald didn't help you to master."

"You may be right," Melanie said. If she were completely honest she would tell how the power of the orgasm had frightened her. She desperately wanted more. She hoped that wasn't a sign of promiscuity. What plagued her thoughts since Winston's love making was how great it felt and how much more she wanted. "If I ever decide to see Winston again, I'll take your advice to talk about pleasing each other."

12

Cruise Days 3 and 4 – Bora Bora

Melanie's note on Bora Bora: Only 4,200 inhabitants live on this jewel of an island framed within a barrier reef with only one water passage that leads into a spacious harbor. Lots of yachts. Used during WWII by American troops for Operation Bobcat. Scuba diver's heaven. Snorkeling with giant manta rays a must do.

"The jog around the island should be nice," Chuck said having breakfast with Winston by poolside. "That line at the treadmill this morning was a joke. Too small a gym for all the healthy people on board."

"Yeah. Shouldn't be too bad a run," Winston said reaching for his glass of water. Chuck and Winston had started jogging together about three years ago. Chuck competed in marathons, but Winston ran just to stay in shape. "It's about five miles to cover this side of the island. Mostly flat roads. I think I'll pick up a lightweight, disposable camera. Capture a few memories of this place to take back."

Chuck nodded. "You're still speaking at the meeting today?"

"They called me this morning. Asked me to participate in several more panel discussions."

"You keep that up, you won't be able to have any fun on this trip. You're not required to be on the panels."

"It's what I do."

"Better you than me," Chuck quipped. "Work typically excites you. So why the grumpy mood? Is something going on?" When Winston didn't answer, Chuck made a mental list of all the possibilities. The list he had come up with started and ended with a woman named Melanie. "I say a female, about five feet seven, pretty, built tight and firm like a brick house, milk chocolate in color." When Winston looked at him, he added. "Probably tastes sweeter than that and you're dying to find out."

"Do you have a point? Or are you trying my patience?"

"Patients?" Chuck deliberately repeated the tired joke. "You got lots of them."

"Get to the point," Winston said flatly.

"Well, you sure seem distracted since you met her. It doesn't take a degree in psychiatry to figure that out. Or that she seems interested in you. I guess your mood means you struck out. Or have you found a Tahitian-flavored honey you're trying to squeeze into this trip?" he grinned.

"Stick to medicine." Winston leaned forward, his elbows on the table and looked out over the pool at Bora Bora. "Fortune-telling isn't your strong suit. And Melanie is *my* business."

"Okay. If you don't want to talk about it, then let's get this morning jog over with." Chuck stood, laughing, not even fazed by Winston's attitude, "That'll give you the think-time to sort out your problem. It's a beautiful day, great breeze. Which should help blow away your confusion. The sooner you figure this out, the better you'll feel."

Winston drank the last of his water and stood up. "Thankfully, you minored in psychology. Else I'd be concerned about your advice."

"Brotha, you got it bad." Chuck grinned, shaking his head. "I'm dropping the topic until you're in a better mood."

The jog around Bora Bora did do the trick. To circle the island was only fifteen miles, but Winston and Chuck used all of the morning to complete the leisurely run, occasionally stopping to enjoy the breath-taking sights. They had started in the village of Vaitape. The stores, hotels, restaurants, banks and post office of which gave it the feel of a small town. Next they headed north along the coastal road, passing the old American World War II base at Faanui Bay. A few coastal guns, a radar station, and a deserted submarine base were the only remnants of a time long ago when the U.S. occupied the area. Further along the bay, they reached Taihi Point where the ruins of a Hyatt hotel stood, a project abandoned years before due to lack of funds. Continuing, they stopped long enough to take pictures of the scenic, quiet, turquoise-colored lagoon on the eastside. From there they went to the south coast, which exploded into an area of hotels and tourist activities where they stopped for a water break. The jog ended at Bloody Mary's, a restaurant famous not only for great food but also the celebrities who often dined there. Chuck noticed the guy who starred in the recent James Bond movie heading inside.

Back at the harbor, they waited to catch the tender back to the ship.

"I'm going to shower then head to the private Motu to lie out under a palm tree for a few hours. I'll be back on board for the meeting tonight," Chuck said. "What're your plans?"

"My plans haven't gotten past taking a shower," Winston said, walking up the gangplank of the ship.

"Still haven't reached any decisions on your problem?" Chuck asked.

"Not yet."

"Well, at least you agree there is a problem," Chuck said before turning to head toward his cabin. "That's a good first step. My minor in psychology makes me an expert on first steps." Chuck grinned widely over his shoulder.

"Bye, Chuck," Winston said sarcastically.

In his cabin, Winston undressed and stepped into the shower. The jog had done a lot of good, even though he hadn't said a word about Melanie to Chuck. The last thing he needed was Chuck riding him about being too attached too soon to the woman. One who lived several states away from his home. And, if Melanie's avoidance of him was a clue, he never would see her again anyway.

Winston didn't like that last thought, but it was clear she was avoiding him. Calling her cabin resulted in zilch. When Sandra answered, Melanie was never available. She wasn't even returning his calls.

The experience they shared in the spa was unbelievable. Making love to her was damn incredible. She had marveled at his caresses, responded passionately to his kisses. She had touched and held him through all of it. It seemed new to her, as if she were making love for the first time, yet she seemed familiar with a man's body, and she had not been timid with him.

She had wanted his touch, responded voraciously to it. Like she needed it, wanted him. Her intense desire for him caressed untouched parts of his soul. The parts that completed him, made him feel whole. And when he honestly reflected on this, he needed to *be* whole. To somehow link the scattered shards of joy he had experienced into one large, enormous chunk of enjoyment. He had allowed himself to give in to the temptation she sparked. And that's what had blown it.

She had made it clear that she didn't want intercourse, had only agreed to allow him to touch her. He had honestly meant to keep it to heavy petting, possibly a massage. But she responded so quickly, eagerly to his touches. And he didn't want to stop himself. He knew he was taking advantage of the situation again. If he had kept his touches less sexually charged, if he had not kissed the private, sweet parts of her, if he had not stroked her until she was too weak to resist, she wouldn't have walked away from him the way she had.

What bothered and intrigued Winston, and what the jog hadn't helped clear up, was her question about having an orgasm. Certainly, sex wasn't new to her. Maybe it was the fact that she had a multiple experience that bothered her.

Being the one to give her that experience should have had him strutting like a peacock. Not a man on the planet wouldn't have had his chest puffed out if a woman reacted like that to his lovemaking. And until she walked away from him, he had felt that way. Even bragged to her. Then she was gone, and he hadn't spoken to her since. The memory of it was so clear; every touch, every word that had passed between them.

She had asked, "What just happened to me?"

He had kissed her, then said, "Sounds to me like you had an orgasm. Possibly two." He stood back admiring her body and added, "You must really like me a lot." He had grinned broadly. "Let's do it again. I want one."

She gave him a look of utter anguish. "This should never have happened," she wailed then walked away from him.

He had followed her into the vanity area. She dressed slowly, as if he wasn't in the room, then turned to him. She looked at his erection then into his eyes, and seemed to want to cry, as she managed to say, "Goodbye, Winston."

"What's wrong?" he had asked, but she opened the door and left. Running after her, nude and penis bouncing for all to see, wasn't the memorable image he wanted to present. So he let her go.

Now, Winston stood allowing the warm water of the shower to clean his body, clear his thinking. He should ask for forgiveness, and promise, yet again, to stop taking advantage of her.

Well, there was one of his problems. He kept breaking his promises to her. He was sure she probably wouldn't forgive him now.

As he stepped out of the shower, another thought came to him. This trip will end on a positive note, he promised himself. Picking up the phone he dialed a familiar number.

"Hello, Sandra. It's Winston. Are you available for lunch?"

13

Melanie had brought her camera's tripod on the trip to use for taking photos of spectacular sunsets. She was on the sun deck, the highest level of the ship, looking for a spot to set it up. She was an amateur photographer, but the classes she had taken ensured that she captured nice enough pictures to use with her articles.

Her research yesterday and today had afforded her plenty of excellent material for this island. She had ended her visit to Bora Bora by sailing around the lagoon on a catamaran with a group from the ship. They sailed north from the township of Vaitape past the airport, and the bungalows of Marlon Brando and Dustin Hoffman. The turquoise lagoon looked refreshingly clean because it was constantly replenished with ocean water from the swells that crashed over the fringe of reefs. In the center of the lagoon was a one sided ancient volcano. Melanie had gotten pictures of it before they docked. Then she and the others swam in the shallow waters of the lagoon for about an hour before returning to town, where she shopped for jewelry made from seashells.

The brilliant day had promised a wonderful sunset and Melanie was excited about taking pictures of it. This was the last day in Bora

Bora and she wanted to capture the sunset as the ship weighed anchor. The view was so perfect, she was sure she would frame some of the pictures to display in her den.

Against the golden setting sun, the blue ocean looked black. After adjusting the filter lenses, Melanie looked up at the lazy sun stretched brilliantly behind a passing cloud in the distance.

Perfect, she thought, *once it moves down as though touching the water I'll take it*. She would wait.

The sun deck overlooked the pool level just below it. On the other side of the pool was the glassed-in patio restaurant and bar, *LeGrill*. She would need to make dinner reservations for 'Al Fresco' tonight if it wasn't too late. Dinner while they sailed along the coast would be nice.

Then she saw a familiar red sundress. Sandra was having cocktails with a man.

Surprise, surprise, Melanie laughed to herself. Though she and Sandra had been friends for ten years, they were complete opposites when it came to men. Sandra was bold, aggressive, outspoken and downright lecherous. Her motto: "Too many men and not enough time."

If Melanie's camera hadn't bee already positioned for the sunset, she would have taken a picture of Sandra leaning close to the man seated next to her. She was pretty in her long, braided hair extensions. The red sundress always enhanced the fullness of her bustline, a treasure she had no qualms in displaying. Her date must have said something funny, because Sandra leaned back, laughing, a hand touching the skin displayed between her treasures.

You better watch out, Melanie thought. *Else Sandra will be reeling you in and dressing you down as tonight's featured catch of the day*. Then the man touched Sandra's hand where it rested on the table. *Maybe he already knew he was caught*, Melanie concluded.

Then they stood up. Melanie lifted her hands to block the sun out of her eye to see if it was Sandra's lawyer friend, or doctor friend or possibly that Indian chief. He was half-blocked by a pole, so she couldn't tell.

Sandra hugged him before they turned toward the pool to leave. It wasn't the lawyer or the Indian chief, Melanie realized. It was the doctor, her doctor, Winston Knight, who embraced her friend, Sandra.

The setting sun kissed the horizon in a perfect display of golden warmth touching an onyx sea. The misty yellow path the sun streaked across the ocean reached all the way to the ship.

It was heaven touching the earth.

Melanie had not captured any of it because she had snatched up her camera and stormed off as her friend and her lover turned and walked arm-in-arm away together.

14

Melanie was seated in the dining area of their cabin sipping a beer when Sandra came breezing in. She hated beer. It was the only form of a sedative in the room's mini-refrigerator. Beer was one of Ronald's favorites, as well as the reason she disliked it so much. She took another sip.

"Hi, Mel!" Sandra said joyously. "Sorry I'm late. You're all changed for dinner. Great hair style. I like it curled and full like that!"

Melanie stood. An image of cold beer running in foamy streaks down red material flashed in her mind. She squelched the desire to fling the beer at Sandra. That, too, was one of Ronald's favorite pastimes.

"Where have you been?" Melanie asked, trying not to sound accusatory. She must have failed, because Sandra gave her a funny look.

"I told you I was going to spend the day on the Bora Bora Motu. I saw Chuck there. We went snorkeling. He's a cutie, but he's playing hard to get. I showered and changed early so I could have drinks with another friend. I've given up on Chuck. There are too many men to be wasting time on one that isn't interested."

"Found someone else then?" Melanie asked, coming to stand next to Sandra.

"I think so," Sandra said as she refreshed her lipstick in the mirror. "Got on my magic dress. It always works!" she joked. "I'm having a drink with him after dinner." She picked up her purse. "Let's get going. We're late. I like that black lace top you're wearing with that skirt. Kinda resembles the top of my sundress, doesn't it?" Sandra opened the cabin door, stepped out and began rushing down the hall. "Girl, hurry up!"

As they reached the pool level, Melanie said to Sandra. "I was looking for you earlier. Someone said they saw you in *LeGrill's*. Were you there to make reservations for us? If so, we're on their book twice." Melanie was probing for the truth, wanting to give her friend a fair chance.

"Nope," Sandra said. "Not at all."

When they reached the entrance to *LeGrill*, Sandra looked around. "Aren't too many people up here. Let's head to the Connoisseur Club for a drink first. Come back in a few minutes. They'll hold our reservation, I'm sure."

Melanie just looked at her. She took a deep breath and decided she would deal with Sandra's deception here and now rather than in the crowded club. "Sandra, the thing I've enjoyed most about our friendship is that I could always count on your honesty and trust. It was one of the things that helped me to get through the mess with Ronald." She bit back the urge to cry. "You were my best friend, even then. Never lied to me in all that time…or at least that I'm aware of…"

"Look, Mel, let's talk about Ronald later." Sandra walked around her, heading toward the Connoisseur Club. "Let's cut through the back way. I need that drink."

"Sandra," Melanie said walking fast to catch up, but she had already stepped back inside the ship's interior hall and was nearing the entrance to the club. "Sandra!" Melanie grabbed her arm. "I saw you in *LeGrill* with Winston. Let's go back outside. I want to talk about why you lied to me, but I don't want to do it in front of a crowd in the club."

"So what!" Sandra pulled away and opened the door. "All's fair in love and war. And I thought you said you weren't interested in him. If you want to talk, I'll be inside the club."

"Fine." Melanie stormed past her and into the Connoisseur Club. *So be it,* she thought. *This discussion will just have to have an audience.*

The Connoisseur Club was empty and Melanie was glad. She wanted to scream and shout. Then it dawned on her that the club hadn't opened for service. Sandra's mistake and lust for alcohol would give her the privacy to deal with this.

Whirling around, she faced Sandra. "Who the hell do you think you are?" Out of the corner of her eye, she spotted movement and was more pissed that the cleaning staff picked this moment to come set up the room.

Sandra looked past Melanie and said, "Not a minute too soon."

Melanie turned slowly, "Winston?" She looked back over her shoulder. "Sandra?"

"Winston," Sandra said. "You better make damn good on your promise to me. I lied to Melanie to get her here. Don't make me regret it!" She turned to leave, but before she did Melanie saw wetness in her eyes.

Winston stopped behind her, but Melanie refused to turn around.

"I needed to see you, Melanie. This was the only way I figured I could. I didn't want to deceive you."

"Melanie stared at the door ahead of her; the door from which her friend had just exited. Sandra was trying to fix things, not break them, she realized.

"If I could start over with you," Winston continued. "I would change several things that have happened. Including this crazy plan." Winston stepped closer, the back of her touching him from chest to thigh. "But a lot I would leave exactly the same."

Melanie fought for the strength to turn and face him. None came. Emotions, all confusing to her, tumbled around her insides: Anger, jealousy, frustration, sadness, envy, and embarrassment. But the one emotion that managed to bubble to the top was the one she honed in on. Relief.

Relief that her friend hadn't deceived her, relief that Winston hadn't abandoned her, and relief that her plans for an enjoyable trip weren't completely lost. And finally, relief mixed with hope, that maybe, just maybe, she would be given a chance to love Winston.

"Winston, I..." she bit back the urge to cry, "I'm...." ur

He turned her to face him.

"I don't know why I'm here," she said to his chest.

"Because I talked Sandra into bringing you here," he said. "I couldn't go another night without seeing you, Melanie."

That did it. She was going to cry and couldn't do a thing about it. She hid her face in her hands.

"I'm sorry," she whispered. "I have something in my eye."

"Tears," he said softly. "Because I hurt you."

"No." She wiped them away and looked up. "They're tears because I hurt you more."

He smiled. "And just how do you think you hurt me?"

"We agreed to be direct and honest with each other," she said. "If I had had the courage to deal with you directly, you would not have stooped to bribing my friend in order to talk to me."

"You're delightful, you know," he said. "Your honesty is so refreshing. So is your smile." He caressed her arms. "I said I wouldn't change a few things. What you just said, I'm adding to the list."

"What?" she asked.

"You just told me you care enough about me that you're crying because you thought you had hurt me."

"I shouldn't feel this way about you," Melanie said, shaking her head.

"Why not?"

"It's too soon. You don't really know me."

Winston wiped a lone tear from her cheek. "I know enough to care about you. Very much. Sandra told me you weren't happy with Ronald."

"Oh did she?" Melanie asked, knowing Sandra wouldn't have revealed the ugliness. But she wondered what she had revealed. "What does that have to do with anything?"

"You went to high school and college with him before you married. I'm not sure why it ended, but she indicated it wasn't pleasant for you because of the things you had discovered about him. You spent almost ten years of your life with him. Do you feel you really knew all that you should have during that time?"

"No." She shook her head.

Winston looked deeply into her eyes. "I think time is relevant to how it's used. I want to make the most of it with you." Then he pulled her close and pressed his mouth to hers.

Melanie opened her lips slowly. His invading tongue assaulted her senses. She reached around him, holding him tightly. The kiss deepened. He tasted of wine and the elation you'd feel when finding your way after being lost.

"Melanie," he said low and husky. "You make me want to try."

"Try what?" she said looking into eyes that reflected too much emotion.

"Falling in love."

His statement stunned her. Then she reached around him for a quick hug before she took a step back. "I...we...." She looked at the exit door.

"Don't run away," he said. "I'm just making an observation about what I'm feeling. I promised to be open and honest with you. Remember?"

Melanie stopped mostly because she needed to know more. "You said earlier that you wished you could change things that had happened between us."

"Some I wouldn't," he added. "Because I like those memories just as they are. Like the way you touch me." He stepped closer and reached for her hands. He kissed the backs of them. "How you held me the first time we kissed on the plane. The dance; definitely not the dance." He laughed. "Your singing...wellllll? I'm not too sure if that makes the list."

"What you have on the list is good," she said, smiling.

"But not complete." Winston let out a soft breath. "I've replayed in my mind the time we spent in the spa. Up until the point when you walked away, it was almost perfect."

She looked at his chest. "I'm sorry about that."

"You can make it up to me by dancing with me," he said.

"Okay," she said smiling. "I'll make it up to you. But I'm not going to sing after that last comment."

Winston led her to the dance floor.

"Wait here." he walked to the door on the other side of the club, spoke to someone on the other side of it and then returned with a man.

"Melanie, this is Hal, the ship's pianist."

"Hello, Hal," she said, the soft lighting making the onyx beads of her lace top shine. Her black flowing skirt moved gently as she took another step toward the piano.

"Winston said you have a request?" Hal took a seat. "What's your pleasure?"

Obviously, Winston had asked Hal to be there for this moment, and that warmed Melanie. "Something nice and slow," Melanie said, looking back at Winston. He was elegant in his navy blazer with gold buttons and taupe slacks.

"What about the theme from Titanic? Celine's song?" Hal said.

"I distinctly remember that ship sinking," Winston said coming to stand in front of Melanie. "And right now sinking ships aren't what I want to think about."

"It wasn't the musicians fault it sank," Hal said jokingly. "You have another suggestion?" He winked at Melanie.

"I prefer *What a Wonderful World*. Louie's song," Winston said, taking Melanie into his arms. "It's my favorite."

"I like that one, too," she said.

As Hal began playing, Winston pulled her closer. "Dance with me," he said softly in her ear. He marveled at her softness, how nicely she fit in his arms as they swayed to the beat of the piano medley.

15

The dance was over. They needed to talk.

Winston invited her back to his stateroom so they could do so in private. Melanie suggested they order room service and talk over dinner.

"Last chance to opt out for more elegant dining," he said, unlocking the door to his cabin.

"I'm dining here tonight, expecting cozy comfort," Melanie smiled.

As they entered the room, she took in the design as Winston turned on lights. It was twice the size of her cabin, more like a small apartment. There was a living room, complete with a sofa, coffee table and two chairs. The dining room seated four, and just beyond a well-equipped kitchen. The bedroom was down a short hall. The balcony, furnished with patio furniture, looked out over a calm ocean.

"Very nice," she said.

"At home, my day starts better having had a cup of coffee on my patio. Just made sense to wake up to one on the ship."

He removed his jacket and placed it on a hanger in the closet, while Melanie telephoned room service.

Winston moved to the sofa and patted the couch next to him when she hung up. "Join me." She did, pulling her legs up on the sofa as she turned to face him. "I didn't mean to cause problems between you and Sandra tonight," he said.

"I caused that. I wouldn't have come into the club if Sandra hadn't said the things she said. She knew that."

"Do you regret her helping?"

"No," Melanie looked at her folded hands in her lap. "I would have avoided you the rest of the trip. Sandra knew that as well."

"Why do you have reservations?" Winston asked.

"I had spent so much time caring for someone who only wanted to cause me pain. It's hard to imagine anything else."

"I can understand that," Winston said. "It was like that with my father. I just don't allow him to make the rules for me anymore."

"Is that why you're so driven? To make better rules for yourself?" Melanie asked.

"Maybe," Winston said before looking at the artwork on the wall in front of him. It appeared as though he was reflecting on the past. "Maybe it is."

"You seem like a man who doesn't know how to fail. Or if you do, then you don't let failure control you. You overcome it. My ex-husband didn't have that ability."

"Did you leave him because of his failures?" Winston asked, looking back at her.

"I divorced him because he punished *me* for them."

Winston considered that, then said, "What was the most important thing you wanted with that relationship and didn't get?"

"Honesty."

"And number two?" he asked.

"Allowing me to be the best I could be," she said. "I like the Melanie I've become. For a while, I didn't think I was worthy of him. I guess I got what I'd asked for."

"I like this Melanie also." Winston reached for her hand and held it in his lap. "And I won't break your number one or number two rule."

"That's nice to hear," she sighed contentedly.

"What else do you want to know about me?" Winston asked.

She thought about it. "Why is it that a good-looking, fine, intriguing. . . ." She thought about other words to describe him but because of his wide grin, she decided those were enough. "Did I say handsome?"

"No," he said.

"I did, too!" She laughed. "I was just testing you. Honestly, men and their egos," she said, shaking her head. "I would think that a woman would have swept you away by now. Or that several of them were in line hoping to."

"Swept away?" Winston repeated. "There's no one of consequence in my life. I thought once or twice I had found someone, but it became obvious that the broom they were using to sweep me away was also their favorite form of transportation."

"You're so funny!" Melanie laughed. "That bad? Witches?" He nodded.

"I love your laugh." Winston slowly pressed her backward so she was lying on the sofa. "It's so genuine. Like you are." He positioned himself gently atop her and kissed her mouth, her neck and the delicate skin above the material covering her breasts. He laid his head on her chest.

Melanie wrapped her arms around him, thrilled by the feel and smell of him. His scent was a spicy cologne mixed with a hint of vanilla, the islands' favorite ingredient for soap.

"If you could relive one moment of your past because it was extremely precious to you, what would it be?" Melanie asked.

"Childhood or adulthood?"

"Most memorable."

He thought about it. "The day my baby sister, Ashley, was brought home from the hospital."

"Why is that?"

"When I was six, my father came home one night from the hospital. He told me I had a sister and that my mother wouldn't be coming home ever again. She had died giving birth. The next morning he brought Ashley home. He said I wouldn't be alone anymore. She had grabbed my fingers and held tight. Somehow it made that day so much better. Memorable."

"I'm sorry," she whispered.

"It was a long time ago. I didn't know how to mourn at that age, but I do remember mornings were lonely without Mom."

Melanie kissed his forehead as she tightened her hold on him. "Are you and your sister close?"

"Very," Winston said. "She lives in LA. I'm going to spend a week with her before going home. She says she has a big surprise for me. I don't have a clue as to what."

There was a rap on the door.

"Dinner's here," Melanie said when Winston didn't move immediately.

Reluctantly, he stood, stuffing his shirttails into the waist of his pants. "Coming!" he said when the rapping continued. He turned back to her. "Before I forget. Thanks for being understanding tonight."

She smiled, then whispered, "My pleasure."

They enjoyed dinner in the silence of two people in love. They didn't need words; their eyes and occasional soft touches spoke volumes in the coziness of the softly lit balcony. After dinner, they sat sipping wine as the ship slowly cruised along the coast.

"Having fun?" Melanie asked, sitting with her bare feet resting on one of the lower railings of the balcony.

"Having peace," Winston said standing. "Let's go inside."

When she rounded the table and came to stand next to him, he took her hand and led her to the bedroom.

Until that moment, Melanie had felt comfortable with him and with herself. She didn't want to go into the bedroom because that meant having sex. She was no good at it and didn't want to ruin their evening.

"Winston?" She said stopping. He looked back. "I was...Can..." she looked into the dark bedroom. He folded his arms across his chest and stood silently, as she considered the best way to tell him she didn't want to disappoint him tonight. "Can we just cuddle?"

"I was hoping you would say something like that." He stepped inside and turned on a light, which barely illuminated the room. He took off his shoes and socks then climbed into the center of the bed. Lying on his back, he placed his hands under his head.

Melanie stood at the side of the bed. Because of the dim lighting she couldn't tell if his eyes were open. But the angle of his head indicated that he was looking at her. She needed to know.

Leaning, she turned on a table lamp then crawled in bed next to him, lying on her side, her head on the pillow next to his arm.

"Did you finish your research?" he asked softly.

"What?" Melanie leaned up on an elbow. Research was the farthest thing from her mind and it took her a few seconds to figure out what he was talking about. "Oh...yes. I got all I need about Bora Bora. Did you tour any of it?"

"Chuck and I jogged around the island the first day. Well, it started as a jog, but we ended up walking and touring. Today, we jogged up and down the harbor side. Picked up trinkets and a few gifts."

"Did you find it to be charmingly sophisticated, warm and friendly. The interior so beautiful and the outskirts so inviting."

Winston reached up and caressed her cheek with the back of his hand, starting at her brow and slowly moving down to the corner of her mouth.

"Yes," he finally said as he drank in her lovely features. He reached for her hand and placed it on his chest. Slowly she moved her hand back and forth, as he exhaled a pleasurable sigh. She wanted to make it happen again. Looking at his closed eyes, she asked. "How do you like to be touched?"

He turned to her. "Any way you want."

"Yes, but," she said, searching for the best phrase, "What turns you on? What do you really like?"

"You touching me as often as you can, with as many parts of your body as possible."

Melanie undid his buttons of his shirt. With the lights on, she watched as her hand explored the tautness of his chest, the firmness of his stomach. She loved the sprinkling of hair that encircled his small nipples and traveled down his stomach before disappearing under his pants. Following that trail, her fingers disappeared as well.

"Mmmmmmm," Winston groaned deeply, and that excited her.

She moved her hand across the material covering his manhood and squeezed.

"I like that," he said.

Melanie wanted to touch more of him, experience more of his reactions to her touch. She wanted to touch his legs with hers. She started to move, but her foot was caught in the fullness of her skirt. That was not going to stop her from touching as much of him with as much of her as she could. She climbed out of bed.

The sleeveless, black beaded bodysuit she wore fit more like a swimsuit. And for that reason she wasn't uncomfortable in wearing it by itself. Standing, she bent and pushed the skirt down her hips, over her thighs to the floor.

"God, Melanie." His voice was raspy.

Slightly bent, she looked back over her shoulder. He was staring at her backside. Her bodysuit fit like a thong and he was enjoying the sight of her. She had become numb to having a man enjoy something as simple as watching her take off her clothes. Ronald had just wanted her naked and in bed. Frilly under things weren't a consideration. Ronald would crawl atop her sometimes dressed, and mostly drunk. Five minutes later it was over. Numbness had been a survival technique.

All men aren't like Ronald, she told herself firmly. *And Winston desires me.* She would change this situation to her benefit.

Slowly turning, she allowed him to enjoy the view of more of her body. Crawling back into bed, she rested on her knees as she looked directly into his eyes.

"Have you forgotten your request to cuddle?" he asked.

"I haven't forgotten. Can you take off your pants?"

"Should I forget?"

"No." She grinned at that. "I want to touch more of your body."

Standing, he removed his pants and tossed them on a nearby chair. Returning to stand facing her, he linked his thumbs in his briefs. "Anything else?"

She could do this! "Those, too," she said and watched, in appreciation, as his body was fully revealed to her. All of him was firm and beautiful.

Winston got back in bed and lay in front of her. Melanie lay on her side facing him. She leaned over and kissed his lips as her hand caressed his chest. The more she touched him, the deeper, more demanding his kiss became.

"Do you like this?" she asked.

"Yes," he said against her mouth as he reached to pull her hips toward his erection.

She kissed his cheek, the side of his face; she rubbed her lips on his ear. "How do you like to be kissed?" she whispered.

"The way you've been doing it."

"Not your mouth." She looked into his eyes as her hand moved between his legs and gently encircled his manhood.

He reached up with both his hands and pulled her mouth to his. His tongue danced with hers, dipped and tasted the top, the corners of her lips. He sucked her tongue before holding it between his teeth. Moving his head slowly back and forth he continued to suck. Melanie gave in completely to the powerful sensations the kiss aroused in her. She moaned and demandingly returned the kiss, suckling, tasting, licking.

He pulled back. "Just like that."

Melanie kissed his neck then moved her lips down to his chest where she sucked his small nipples. His moans were reassuring. She continued down to his stomach, tasted his navel. All of him smelled of spice and vanilla making her want to nibble all his skin. The more she tasted, enjoyed, the more Winston moaned and sighed.

"OOOOhhhhhh, Melanie!" he grunted when her mouth closed around the tip of his manhood and tantalizingly caressed. "Yes... That's...so...good..." Then she moved faster. He reached for her. "Don't...Or...I'll..." She continued her assault, ignoring his pleas because she knew how much pleasure she was giving him. The more she tasted; the more he enjoyed it. "Mel..." He reached for her.

Then he burst into pieces of exhilaration, spilling into utter pleasure. As he trembled from the climax, she kissed him softly all the way up his body to his mouth.

"Did you like that?" she softly asked.

"God, yes." His breathing was labored.

"Not too bad for a first time, huh?"

He stared at her. "Baby, you're incredible."

She lay on top of him and held him, feeling his labored breathing against her chest. He was so warm and so pleased, and it was because of her.

This was good, she thought.

Winston wrapped his arms around her and hugged her tightly.

As they lay in each other's arms, the ship moved smoothly toward Moorea Island, lulling them to sleep.

16

Days 5 and 6, Moorea Island

Melanie's notes on Moorea: It's ruggedly mountainous. The 11,000 inhabitants range from rural farmers to the elite. Coffee, coconut and pineapple plantations are plentiful. Pulp of Noni fruit shipped to America. Noni pulp is full of nutrients, reinforces immune system and slows tumor growth. One hospital here and it services other islands (Raiatea and Tahaa). Famous Cook's Bay named after British Captain James Cook, who was the first European to visit the islands of Huahine, Tahaa, and Raiatea. Hollywood's Mutiny on the Bounty *filmed in Moorea. Beautiful Protestant and Catholic churches.*

Winston and Chuck sat by the pool having breakfast. Winston hadn't seen Melanie since he fell asleep holding her. He woke up this morning to a note that indicated she needed to do some reading before attending the onboard presentation on 'Ancient Mysteries, Medicines and Gods of Tahiti.' Then she was going parasailing before heading to shore.

He didn't like Melanie just leaving him, not saying goodbye. He felt alone—a feeling he no longer wanted. He would have to tell her that she should wake him in the future.

But then the note ended with the part he liked the most. He smiled. Melanie had asked to have dinner with him tonight.

"I'm looking forward to the dive trip to The Ledges this afternoon. I hear the coral reef extends more than 200 feet," Chuck said.

"I can do without the sharks on this dive. They're more plentiful near this island than at Bora Bora."

"That's because they're always feeding the damn things," Chuck offered. "Did you see the write up about diving while they feed them?"

"I hope they meant feeding them fish not scuba divers." They laughed. Winston said, "After the dive, I'm headed to Moorea. I'm not going to the medical meeting tonight."

"Whoa!" Chuck said, surprised. "I think you're serious. You're on the panel for this meeting."

"I want to enjoy some of the island tonight," Winston said. "I was thinking of spending the night at one of those hotels that have those grass huts on stilts sitting out over the lagoon. They're called overwater bungalows, but the rooms have all the luxuries of an upscale hotel. The flooring is part glass so you can watch the sea life. I think that it would be something damn...." Winston stopped himself from saying "romantic" and added, "interesting." He sliced a piece of pineapple.

Chuck started laughing. "Have you just realized that there's more to life than work? Or are you having a flashback of the last dive with the shark?"

"The thing bumped into me. The shark looked more surprised than I did. And it was only three feet long."

"Then what?" When Winston didn't answer, but sliced into a melon instead, Chuck revisited his top-ten list of things that might be distracting Winston. "I still say female, about five-feet-seven, skin reminds you of milk chocolate, face of an angel with a hell of a body. But you've had a taste and decided to have that sweet thing's sweet thing again."

"I still say your career as a psychic is going straight to hell."

"And I say you're full of sh...." Chuck was interrupted by a high-pitched shriek.

"Dr. Knight!" It was Ethel Hightower, with her husband in tow, coming their way.

"Good morning, Mrs. Hightower," Winston said. "You remember Dr. Rogers."

"Absolutely! Good morning to you both. Bill and I have been having the best fiftieth! I must say...." And she did. At record speed she recapped their tours on Raiatea and Tahaa. And how the snorkeling on the Motu was absolutely breathtaking. Actually, it had taken her breath away when she had swallowed too much water and almost drowned. But she managed to put her feet down in the three-foot water, coughed herself back to life, then continued with her snorkeling adventure.

When Winston and Chuck were about to mentally fade out of the discussion, it got interesting.

Surprisingly so.

"I heard the marvelous news, Dr. Knight." Mrs. Hightower's whisper was still too loud for Winston when she added, "about your marriage onboard! Did the captain do it? You know they're licensed for those sorts of things!"

Chuck looked at Winston, who hurriedly picked up his orange juice.

"Who told you that lie?" Chuck asked when Winston kept drinking.

"It was the talk at the dinner table last night," Mrs. Hightower said, offended at being called a liar. "Dr. Miller told all of us about it." She turned her attention back to Winston. "And that your wife is a famous writer!"

"Mrs. Hightower," Winston finally said, "Melanie and I didn't get married on this ship. We aren't…."

"I thought so!" Mrs. Hightower interrupted. "I told Bill," she patted her husband's arm, "that I thought you did it on the island. It's more romantic that way! That's the exact same way we renewed our vows on our twentieth." Mrs.. Hightower bent and attempted another too-loud whisper. "But the ring, Dr. Knight? I'm thinking you could have done more with the wedding ring. Especially since we're in the land of black pearls!" Mrs. Hightower's excitement was growing. "Diamonds and a black pearl would be fitting for an island ring! I'm an expert on pearls and have examined some of the ones at the shops on the islands. The nacre thickness is extremely important. And then there's the shape. Perfectly round and pear shaped are rare. They only make up two percent of all that are harvested. I was telling…"

"Mrs. Hightower?" Winston said, standing. He needed to shut her up.

"Yes, Dear?"

"I didn't pick out the ring Melanie is wearing either. She's been attached to it since the moment we met." Winston figured that much was the absolute truth. He had noticed the ring the moment he had seen her at the airport.

"Sentimental value possibly," Mrs. Hightower concluded.

"I was wondering if you could help me with picking out a ring for Melanie, since you know so much about them. Moorea probably has a shop where we can get one. Would you consider helping..."

"Absolutely, Dear!" Mrs.. Hightower brightened. "I just knew you had a perfect explanation!" She went into deep thought, slowing her speech. "I say. This should take some careful planning with you on your honeymoon and all. I better go scout out some places today, then take you to see my choices."

"I really do like that idea," Winston said.

Mrs. Hightower beamed again. "We need to go. Bill," she looked at her husband, "didn't I tell you Melanie and Dr. Knight would be perfect together?"

Winston and Chuck looked at Mr. Hightower. He was using a celery stick to chase an ice cube around the glass of what looked like a long gone Bloody Mary. Hightower tipped up the glass and downed the ice, the final drops of tomato juice and vodka. He crunched on the celery stick as if attempting to get more drink from it. He looked in their general direction and smiled. Winston assumed that was as close to an answer they were going to get.

"Bill and I," Mrs. Hightower said regaining their attention, "are off to do your bidding!"

"Winston?" Chuck asked, watching Mrs. Hightower head across the ship, stopping to chat with all in her path. "Do you think there's a cure for that woman's mouth? I don't think it can close."

Laughing, Winston sat back down.

"Married now?" Chuck asked him.

"You know that I'm not," Winston said, reaching for his juice. "Melanie was called Mrs. Knight at dinner. She never corrected the error and now it's grown."

"So Melanie also wants people to think you're married?"

"Not exactly. She said she would correct the rumor. I'm letting her handle it."

"According to motor-mouth, the rumor is spreading fast. And the assignment you just gave her won't help matters."

"The rumor is limited to this ship. No harm done."

Chuck folded his arms across his firm chest and looked pointedly at Winston. Then he mentally amended his list about Melanie. "This explains a few things."

"I'm sure you're planning to tell me all of them," Winston said flatly.

"If you insist." Chuck placed his elbows on the table. "You've just taken her off the market. Remember Charles?" When Winston nodded, he continued. "Charles mentioned he was interested in her, but changed his tune last night at dinner. Said something about her being happily married."

"If Charles pays attention to his wife like he does other women, he wouldn't be having marital problems."

Chuck ignored that, still adding to his list. "And the looks she gets when she strolls around the pool in that swimsuit would have more guys chasing behind her, but now they think she belongs to you."

Winston didn't comment just looked out over the turquoise water surrounding Moorea Island.

"I wonder what Daphne would say if the rumor ever leaves the ship. She was planning on being Mrs. Dr. Winston Knight."

Winston snapped to attention. "It's over between Daphne and me."

"Is that why you argued with her the night before we left Los Angeles?"

"She was upset because I uninvited her on this cruise. I wasn't going to change my mind at the last minute, either. She wants back into my life, but I'm not interested in that affair. It's too draining."

"So it's over this time?" Chuck asked.

"It was over the first time."

"But does *she* know that," Chuck said. "Now that I think about it, you've been smiling a lot more lately. Because Daphne is gone? Or because Melanie's here?"

"Chuck, let me be honest with you," Winston said, leaning back.

"About time!"

"Melanie is a wonderful change for me. I came here for a getaway, not to get snagged. She knows I'm a doctor. She respects it, and that's all. She cares more about what makes me smile than how much I make. She only wants to please. I need that. I've never had that."

"Then I was wrong," Chuck said. "You don't have it bad; you have it just right. I've heard enough complaints about the women you've dated who drain you. Keep her if you can."

"That's my plan."

"I thought she lived up north some place," Chuck said. "Dakota or Delaware..."

"Denver," Winston corrected.

"That's a lot of commuting for a Friday night date," Chuck said.

"Yeah, Dallas would be the D-word that I'd prefer if I had my way," Winston said.

"So what are you going to do about it?" Chuck asked.

"I not going to lose her," Winston said with finality. "I'll worry about the logistics of it later."

Melanie and Sandra were going down the stairs to Level 3 to catch the tender to Moorea Island. Sandra had decided to spend the day with Melanie researching because she enjoyed the workshop on island myths they had attended that morning. When they reached Level 3, the elevator in back of them opened and out walked the Hightowers.

"Mrs. Knight!" Mrs.. Hightower called to Melanie, but she kept walking. "Mrs. Knight…*Melanie!"*

Melanie turned. "Hi there." Melanie set her straw hat on her head. "Were you calling me?"

"You really do have to get used to your new name, Dear!" Mrs. Hightower explained. "Are you headed to shore now?"

"No!" Sandra butted in wanting to avoid the ride with the Hightowers. The tender had a top and bottom level and could seat at least forty people comfortably, but Sandra didn't want to take a chance on being seated next to them and hear all that yapping, especially with her hangover. Tenders left just about every twenty minutes, and if necessary, she and Melanie would wait for the next one. "We're not leaving yet!"

"That's too bad," Mrs. Hightower said. "What's your ring size, Dear?"

"Seven. Why?"

"Oh, nothing! Your husband asked that I do some investigating for him. I just wanted to confirm a few things first. And your favorite color?"

"Yellow. What husband? I'm not married."

"Poor, Dear," Mrs. Hightower sympathetically shook her head as she patted Melanie's arm. "I had the same problem too with remembering at first. But after fifty years you can't forget!"

"But I'm divorced." Melanie said

Sandra's question was said even louder. "Who is she married too?"

"You haven't heard about the romantic private wedding they had on the island? It was absolutely beautiful. Dr. Knight told me all about it. I'm sure Melanie will tell you all the details. I must go. The tender is about to leave. Dr. Knight is a great doctor. And I'm sure he'll be a wonderful husband. Toodeloo!" Then she was gone.

Sandra and Melanie watched the Hightowers make their way to the tender station, past security, then down the stairs to the boat.

"Melanie, I know you were mad and considered renegotiating our friendship because I helped Winston, but I thought I would at least be in your wedding!"

"Sandra, *I* wasn't even in the wedding!"

"Diarrhea-mouth just said...." Sandra considered the source, then sobered. "I'm sure her husband was lit. Every time I've seen him he's got a drink in his hand. But his wife seemed almost sane until now."

"And, according to her, Winston told her we were married," Melanie added.

"He must've been joking!" Sandra said.

"He better have a damn good reason for letting this rumor get out of control."

"You mean you've already heard it?"

"Actually," Melanie corrected. "I sort of started it."

"And I'm sure you have a valid excuse for letting folks believe you're married to the finest man onboard?"

"He's not the finest," Melanie said. "Just the cutest."

"Pardon me?" Sandra crossed her arms. "We have twenty minutes to kill before the next tender. I'm expecting to get all the details on this!"

"Sandra, why do you feel you need to know the latest on everything?" Melanie turned toward the stairs going up. "Let's go to the board games area and work on the jigsaw puzzle for a bit."

"Ever since we opened that box everyone has been working on it." Sandra followed Melanie up the stairs. "It's probably done by now, so you'll have time to chat about marriages and play-play weddings."

"Not much to tell," Melanie said. "One night at dinner some people thought we were married. Probably because we were together and most of them were. Since they're Winston's associates, he should speak to them."

"I see," Sandra said, not really understanding, but it was obvious she wanted to know more about important issues. "Well, why would Mrs. Hightower want your ring size?"

"If you hadn't declined the ride over with them," Melanie said as she headed down the hallway, "we could have found out."

"My hangover and Mrs. Hightower are allergic to each other."

They looked down at the completed puzzle and frowned.

"This one, big happy family stuff on this small ship is getting ridiculous," Sandra whined. "We can't even work on a puzzle all by ourselves."

"Let's swing by the library," Melanie said. "I want to pick up that book on Polynesian myths. I'll drop it off in the room and then we'll head to the island."

On land, they met the private tour guide and went to a village to experience the old, traditional Tahitian ways. Melanie and Sandra watched tikis being carved and the tie-dying of *pareus*—the Polynesian sarongs–using natural ingredients like fruit. In what seemed like record time, they witnessed a woman weave a basket out of coconut palms.

"Let's go over there and watch the men." Sandra tugged at Melanie's arm.

"They're only getting tattoos, Sandra."

"But they're barely dressed. That's the part that makes watching the tattooing enjoyable."

The guide was explaining the ceremony surrounding ancient tattooing as they watched the process. "Tattooing was sometimes followed by human sacrifices in the old days, but not to worry, Miss," he said, grinning at Sandra. "We stopped doing that when the missionaries came to the islands."

"Amen," Sandra said and Melanie laughed.

"The tattoos today are just for show," the guide said, "and are applied with electric needles and China ink. Much faster!"

They also learned about the traditional plants used by ancient Tahitians to make soap out of ginger, sacred oils and also perfumed with sandalwood and candlenut. They had ingredients that were wonderful for adding moisture to the skin.

After watching several dancers move smoothly to the music of men playing guitars and ukuleles, they headed to the jeep.

"I love air conditioning," Sandra said, getting into the backseat. "Turn it up high!"

They went to the eight-sided church built in 1822 by Protestant missionaries. It was the oldest European building still standing on the Society Islands. From there, they went to *Opunohu* Bay before visiting *Belvedere*, a vista point that looked out over dreamy mountains with waterfalls and rolling hills that sloped and peaked, all covered with green vegetation. Driving farther around the fruit-tree-lined bay, they passed a botanical garden and more vanilla and fruit farms.

When the trip was just about to get boring to Sandra, who had seen one too many fruit plantations, they came across an open-air market bustling with people. They stopped to shop for gifts and trinkets.

"The craftsmanship is incredible," Melanie said as she looked at a belt made from shells of the black pearl oysters strung together.

"Buy it!" Sandra said, trying on one. "Actually buy two and give me one!"

Melanie smiled and looked for matching earrings. "Having fun on the educational tour?"

"I am," Sandra admitted.

"St. Joseph's Catholic Church is close by," Melanie said. "I want to get pictures of its altar, the one made from mother-of-pearl."

"Sounds good." Sandra tried on a bracelet.

"What do you think of this dress?" Melanie asked, holding up a colorful sundress of burgundy and golden hues. "Maybe I'll wear it to dinner tonight."

"I like. And so will Winston."

"I had a great time with him last night," Melanie said dreamily. "It feels so good. I can't wait to be with him."

"You need to hurry up and forgive me for butting in!" Sandra said. "You smile every time you talk about him. I'm responsible for that."

"Sandra, when we talked about it this morning, I told you that I wasn't happy with you getting involved, but I'm extremely happy with the way it turned out. And for that reason, I've forgiven you."

"Just didn't make any sense you letting that fine man get away without having more of him." Sandra picked up some earrings.

"Winston has good intentions," Melanie said. "And I do enjoy being with him."

"Well, he *is* your husband!" Sandra burst out laughing. "That's too much how the rumor is going around like it is."

"I never thought about it a second time the night of the mix up. I told Winston to tell his fellow doctors the truth. I guess it slipped his mind."

"I guess." Sandra didn't seem convinced. "But they also think you had an island wedding. Mistaken identity is one thing, but putting events around it is another."

"You know how rumors are. Once they get started. It's like a wild-fire."

"What are you going to say to Winston?"

"That he has to deal with this," Melanie said. "I invited him and Chuck to dinner tonight. You're coming aren't you?"

"You aren't trying to hook me up with Chuck, are you?"

"You don't need me to get you guys," Melanie laughed. "I just thought it would be nice for all of us to have dinner together."

"I'm coming to witness you newlyweds up close," Sandra said, following Melanie to the cashier.

"That's not funny!"

"Rumor had it...."

"Don't tell me you're going to join the rumor mill, too!"

"Me?" Sandra laughed. "'Course not, Mrs. Knight!"

They left the market and headed to the church, then east past Cook's Bay to the aquarium and later to the art gallery called *Galerie Aad Van der Heyde* built in 1970 by a resident artist to showcase his primitive paintings of Pacific art.

They finished their tour and headed back to the bay to catch the tender to the ship. Melanie wanted to nap before dinner. She had expected to spend time with Winston after dinner and didn't want to be too tired for it. The day on Moorea was great, though exhausting. Still she and Sandra planned to have just as much fun at dinner.

17

"A toast!" Sandra held up her glass as she sat at the cozy table for four in *LeVeranda*. "To more great days and better nights!"

"I second that," Chuck said.

Winston and Melanie joined by clinking their glasses with Sandra's and Chuck's. They all sipped.

"And also to new beginnings and false marriages!" Chuck added to the toast.

Melanie promptly began choking and Winston patted her on her back. "Excuse, me," she managed. "I'm okay." She looked up to see Sandra doubled over in laughter. "I'm choking, Sandra, that ain't funny."

"But the rumor is!" Sandra managed to say between chuckles. She stopped long enough to ask, "When are you two going to tell these people the truth?"

"Melanie's handling it," Winston said, scanning his menu.

"Me?" Melanie gasped. "They're your friends and associates! *You* should correct them!"

"If you had dealt with it when Dr. Poole got the wrong idea, it wouldn't have gotten out of control."

"You were there too!" Melanie said. "You had just as much opportunity as I had."

Sandra laughed harder. She looked at Chuck, who was also laughing, and said, "Awwwww! Ain't that sweet? Married only one day and fighting like an old married couple!"

Melanie found it hard to find something to grin at but Chuck sure didn't. "Counseling a must!" he added. "I have a friend, a doctor of course, who might be able to help you two out!"

"I guess the honeymoon is over!" Sandra added.

"You mean it started already?" Chuck responded.

"Look," Sandra found her voice again. "This woman stopped me earlier wanting to know if Melanie wore the traditional exotic flowers as a bridal headdress." Sandra wheezed before adding, "I almost forgot she was pretending to be married. But I had to tell the woman something. I had to make up something. So I told her that Melanie went with the bamboo and banana leaf look. More modern!"

"Banana leaves are as tall as I am, Sandra!" Melanie said pleadingly. "How could I possibly wear them on my head."

"You know I'm not good at making up stuff on the spur of the moment! She seemed impressed! I think she thinks you walked down the aisle with bananas hanging around your ears. Wait 'til the gossip mill gets hold of that!"

Sandra and Chuck started laughing again. Sandra dabbed at tears while Chuck slapped his thigh. Melanie and Winston couldn't help themselves. They soon joined in the laughter.

"These people have too much extra time on their hands," Sandra said. "I don't understand it. I'm busy from the time I get up in the morning until I pass out at night. I didn't even know a rumor was out until Melanie told me today."

"This ship is small," Melanie said. "Everyone meets everyone at least twice."

"I guess," Sandra said, "But, Lord....

The waiter came to the table. "Mr. and Mrs Knight?" He placed a bottle of champagne on the table. "Mr. Carpenter and his wife send their congratulations to you."

The laughter started all over again.

"Thanks for asking me to dinner," Winston said as he and Melanie walked down the corridor of Level 6.

"You mean the comedy show we just left?" Melanie said as they reached the elevator. "Sandra and Chuck laughed at us the entire time."

Stepping inside, he pressed the button for Level 3.

"We're leaving the ship?"

"Yes," he said. When the doors reopened, he led the way to the tender station. "Feel like a movie tonight?"

"In Moorea? They don't have movie theaters."

"I have connections," Winston said, heading down the steps. "And it's my treat."

"Okay!"

Melanie wore the burgundy and gold sundress she had bought that afternoon. The night's breeze blew the soft material around her calves as they stood at the shore waiting for a cab. Winston smiled. She was a picture perfect ad for the islands.

After getting settled into a cab, Winston gave the driver the destination in French. Then he turned to Melanie. "I'm having a great time. Thanks."

"I'm glad." She snuggled close to him.

The cab stopped at a hotel entrance and Melanie got out first. "These are bungalows, Winston, not the movies. Are we lost?"

"Stop complaining," he grinned. "I rented the place this afternoon. Comes with all the comforts of a movie and home."

They walked down the softly lit, winding wooden dock. Several large huts, built on stilts, sat over the aqua waters of the bay. Marine life frolicked beneath them under the glow of the lights.

"We're here," Winston said, unlocking the door to one of the huts.

"How lovely!" Melanie said.

The flooring was hardwood with a glass center. Melanie looked through it, to see the ocean creatures. The walls were lined with a material that reminded her of thick parchment. The furnishings were made from bamboo and wood. Bright tropical colors brightened bedspread and curtains.

"They are nice," Winston agreed, turning on the television.

"I visited a pearl farm on Bora Bora," she said. "I had to take a boat to it. The huts looked a lot like this one on the outside with the palm leaves for a roof, but nothing compared to this on the inside."

Winston picked up the videotape and turned on the VCR. "Movie. As promised."

"Great! What are we watching?"

"It's *Mutiny on the Bounty* starring Marlon Brando. Filmed here in Moorea in 1962. Have you seen it?" When she said no, he added, "Let's try to find spots we've been to in the movie."

"Sounds like fun," Melanie said as he started the movie. "I read that Brando bought an island and built a home out here after falling in love with his Tahitian co-star in the movie. We'll have to rate their love scenes. Let's see if we can tell if he's just acting or having a good time."

"Good idea," Winston said joining her on the bed.

They cuddled to watch the movie, which reenacted the actual mutiny that took place on Captain Bligh's ship, the 'Bounty,' and the way the twenty-four mutineers under the guidance of Fletcher Christian took over the ship in 1789. They loved the Polynesian islands more than they did their captain, so after they seized the ship they traveled back to recapture the bliss they had found there. The ending, more Hollywood liberties than reality, was tragic but touching.

As the credits rolled, Winston took his last sip of pineapple juice. "That wasn't too bad. I've seen some of those mountain views before. What did you think of the love scenes?"

Melanie turned to him. "Some seemed real to me. He loved her in real life."

Winston switched off the television, and the sounds of soft waves running to shore played in the distance.

"This was a nice idea."

"Something damn romantic is what it is," Winston said and Melanie starting laughing.

"I remember Sandra telling you to do that," she said.

He got back in bed beside her. "So you *were* in the room when I called looking for you?"

"Yes," Melanie wrapped her arms around him when he leaned over her. "But that was long ago, when I didn't think we should be spending time together."

"And now?"

"I want to enjoy you while I have you," she said.

"Melanie, what do you want to happen with us when we return to the real world?"

"Do you want to try to continue what we've started?" she asked.

"We live over a thousand miles apart," he said. "My practice is thriving in Dallas. You've managed to work out a plan with the university in Boulder that allows you to teach but still have the freedom to pursue your passion to write. It seems like we both have obligations that will keep us apart."

"I've thought about this," Melanie admitted, "but I haven't figured out anything."

"Do you want it to end between us?" he asked softly.

Melanie smiled at him. "It's interesting how you ask questions without having to admit anything about what you want." She leaned up and kissed him softly. "I'll open up first. Because it sounds like you're searching for something."

"I am," he said gazing into her eyes. "I want to know how you feel about me."

"I hoped it was obvious. But I know better than anyone that actions and words need to go together." She exhaled slowly. "I want you, Winston. I want there to be an us. But I'm not going to demand anything you aren't willing to give to me. I have feelings for you but I don't know how to interpret them."

"Why not?"

"I had spent almost ten years loving a man. But I discovered, after the fact, it was never really love. I was looking to be the perfect girlfriend, the best bride, the wholesome wife. But that didn't define me. It was just a part of who I had become. I found my true self after leaving him, but that made me question what I believed about caring for someone. I thought love was being what the other person wanted you to be. I don't believe that now."

"What is it then?" Winston asked.

"To me?" she said reflecting, "It's feeling as though you complete something that is more than you are. That I can be myself when I'm with someone. I take all of me and add to him. I don't take away, nor do I need him to feel complete. It's the togetherness that makes us better than ourselves. And through that, something special should grow." She looked back at him. "Does that sound as confusing as I believe it did?"

"I think I understand," he said smiling. "You want to be able to willingly share all of yourself with someone."

"Yes," she said.

"And you want him to love you for who and what you are."

"Yes," she laughed. "You do this better than I do."

"No I don't," Winston said. "I wouldn't have said any of it if you hadn't inspired the thoughts."

"Winston?" she asked softly. "Can I ask you something? And I want you to be honest with me."

"Always."

"Is it okay if I fall in love with you?" she asked.

He fell silent. He placed his mouth to her chest and exhaled his warmth through her skin and into her heart. Then he lay his head to listen to her heartbeat. Melanie didn't repeat her question nor did she feel he was ignoring her. He needed time. Long minutes later he turned his head and kissed the skin covering her heart. Moving up, he kissed her brow, then her temple, then her cheek.

Looking down at her he said, "I would like that." He kissed her lips. "Because I've already started to fall in love with you."

Melanie wrapped her arms around his neck and kissed him deeply. The more she kissed him, the more she wanted him. "Let's cuddle."

"We *are* cuddling," he grinned.

"You know what I mean!" she said. "You just want me to ask outright."

"Ask."

"Okay." The new Melanie was comfortable with who she was and could speak her thoughts. "Do me a favor and let me make love to you?"

"Sure," he said laughing. "I love the way you ask questions." He got out of bed and took off his shirt. Reaching into his pocket he pulled out several condoms. "It was careless before by not having one of these handy. That's not like me."

"Okay," she said taking the foiled packet. "Winston?" she said and he turned to her. Melanie sat up and swung her legs over the side of the bed, toes touching the floor. Honesty, she thought. "I want to do it better this time. I know I didn't please you when we were in the spa, but I really would like to try tonight."

He started laughing. "Why do you think you didn't please me?"

"You...didn't..." Melanie pulled at inner strength. This was exposure of a weakness, one that had haunted her for years. She wasn't any good at lovemaking. "Didn't ejac...uhm, cum when we had intercourse. And you told me you didn't. Besides, I saw your erection before I left."

He sat beside her. "Melanie, that's not a major requirement for me to enjoy you. I was satisfied knowing you enjoyed me." Winston thought about it. "Was Ronald the only other man you've slept with?"

"Yes," she whispered.

"Don't use him as our yardstick."

She leaned over and kissed him. "It was never like it is with us." She lay back pulling him into her arms. "And I want you so much."

"You can have me as much as you want. Never deny us this," Winston said. "Indulge your fantasies with me."

They kissed and fondled and undressed each other. When their clothing was gone, she touched as much of his body with as much of hers as she could while Winston kissed down her neck and chest to suck her breast. Lovingly, he teased her nipples, squeezing their roundness and tasting her all over. He parted her legs and teased her hidden treasure with the pads of his fingers. When she called to him, he rammed his full erection and the dance of lust began.

"You please me, Melanie," he whispered in her ear as he slid his hardness around inside her.

They reached their heavenly peak with explosive intensity before spiraling back down to Earth, to the bed, together. The sensations waxed and waned, as the sound of lazy waves softly danced along the shore.

18

Cruise Day 7, Papeete, Tahiti

Melanie's notes on Papeete: In 1818, London Missionary Society built the church at the waterfront that helped the port grow in earnest; the Paofai Church now occupies the site. The airport was built in 1961 and launched the now-booming tourism and increased business. Vaima Shopping Center has exquisite boutiques. A must tour: Gauguin Museum, Faarumai Waterfalls, the Taiarapu Penisula, and the impressive Musee de Tahiti et des Iles. Over 130,000 people live in this fast-paced city, which helps prepare travelers for the mindset of the real world. Yet I'm sad…

This was the last day the *Paul Gauguin* would be in Moorea. The ship would leave at six o'clock that evening and dock three hours later in Papeete.

Winston woke up smiling.

The first thing he saw was the bright colors of the bungalow's curtains at the window. Turning, he reached for Melanie and touched paper instead. She was gone and he was alone.

Winston lost his smile; the loneliness dawned.

It was another note of Melanie's and it bothered him. For some reason, she felt it was okay for her to leave him there, alone, to endure the emptiness. And after their lovemaking, it was the last thing he wanted to feel. To squelch the ache, he got up and slipped on the complimentary housecoat. He went out onto the balcony and looked out over the brilliant blue waters surrounding the bungalow. The view, the sound, the breeze brought on the peacefulness he wanted. After several deep breaths he felt much better and smiled. Looking down, sea creatures swam by. He remembered the fish food packets he had brought yesterday and left inside. He had planned to sit with Melanie on the small balcony, sipping coffee, feeding the fish, enjoying each other's company.

But Melanie's note said she had gone out to research and would see him tonight. Winston figured he should stop sulking and start his day as well. He went back inside to shower and dress. He would head back to the ship and hopefully join Chuck for breakfast before going to his onboard medical workshop.

Aboard ship, Winston entered the restaurant and spotted Chuck having breakfast with old Dr. Miller. The man really did look like Father Time.

"Good morning, Dr. Miller," Winston said, walking up to the table. "Chuck." Winston nodded to his friend.

"Join us," Miller said, flashing his dentist's marvelous handiwork. "We were just talking about you."

Winston pulled up a chair. "Care to fill me in?"

"Your input at the workshop meetings has been great," Miller said. "I was just wondering if your honeymoon would continue to prevent you from presenting at the other meetings. At least that's what Dr. Rogers thinks." Miller looked at Chuck.

Winston noticed Chuck's wide grin and looked back at Miller. "I'm planning to speak at the workshop today."

"Great!" Miller enthused. "I think it fascinating how you combine traditional Western medicine practices with Eastern medical wisdom."

"A lot of my patients come to me in great pain," Winston said. "Most have lifestyles that are mentally and physically stressful as well. They need more than just prescription drugs. Self-healing helps."

"The National Institute of Mental Health preaches that seventy percent of all illness is due to stress," Chuck added. "That includes chronic pain conditions. What Winston talks about is ways to release that stress."

"Yes, but what are these Tai Chi and QiGong techniques I hear you're going to talk about today?" Miller asked.

"I'll give the details in the workshop," Winston said. "Are you planning to be there?"

"Depends on what you tell me now," Miller said.

"Tai Chi and QiGong combine specialized breathing techniques with visualization exercises."

"Chuck, I thought you said Winston was going to give pointers for reducing anxiety, depression and mood disturbances," Miller said.

"Those are benefits of Tai Chi and QiGong, but the techniques can also boost the immune system, lower high blood pressure and raise energy," Winston said, taking the menu from the waiter. "I'll have a coffee."

"Deep breathing does all that?" Miller asked, laughing. "I've been away from practicing medicine too long!"

"QiGong means breathing exercise and Tai Chi is slow motion movement," Winston said. "Together you get the benefits."

"QiGong is 2,000 years old," Chuck added. "But the way it can be incorporated today is cutting edge. I had a patient who suffered in pain for years from a whiplash injury, but after a few weeks of Tai Chi her pain disappeared."

"My word!" Miller said. "It makes sense. I guess you might be able to teach this old dog a new trick or two," Miller laughed.

"I'd love to have you at the workshop," Winston smiled, then turned to give his breakfast order to the waiter.

"Count me in," Miller said merrily. After the waiter left he continued, "Mrs. Hightower told me at dinner that you two are going shopping for wedding rings today. I know it's all hush-hush! I'll keep it a secret."

Chuck choked on his coffee, unable to contain his laughter.

"Are you going to be okay?" Miller asked Chuck.

"It's amazing how fast news travel," Chuck managed to say.

"Good news at that!" Miller said. "I hear you had to grab something last-minute for the surprise wedding on the island, but plan on correcting that today."

"I'll see what today brings," Winston said evasively.

He considered correcting the misunderstanding about his nuptials, but figured at this junction no one would believe him anyway. He sipped on his coffee and watched Chuck still trying not to strangle to death on his coffee. Poor Dr. Miller looked confused.

After the workshop, Winston spent the remainder of the day touring and shopping in Moorea and got back in time to catch the last tender to the ship before it departed.

Melanie's note had indicated that he should meet her at poolside at sunset for the ship's departure. He went to his room to drop off the gifts he had brought in Moorea. He wanted to take a shower and change before heading topside. He would also have to pack before meeting Melanie, because luggage would be picked up later that night and stored for tomorrow's disembarkation.

Since they planned to attend the Broadway style show on board tonight, Winston decided on olive-color, cotton slacks and tan button-up shirt. 'Country Club casual' was the ship's mandate for dress code.

Stepping outside on the pool level, Winston looked around for Melanie. She was on the sun deck adjusting her tripod and looking out at the beautiful sunset.

She was wearing another one of those lace tops that he found himself loving. This one was white, and she wore it with a red *pareu* with white flowers wrapped around her waist, fitting like a long skirt. When she saw him, she waved, her loose hair blowing in the wind. She made the perfect picture, he thought, her smile always enthralling.

He stood for several moments appreciating the sight of her. She took the camera off the tripod and aimed it at him. He headed her way.

He had been missing her, had needed to hold her since this morning. *Morning*, he thought, as a spark of annoyance washed over him. He knew he had to fix that problem now. Walking purposely, he headed around the pool, up the stairs, around the sun deck's bar and over to where she stood waiting.

Melanie had repositioned the camera on the tripod. She took a step toward him and threw her arms around his neck. "I was just thinking about you." She kissed him quickly. "It's funny how I sometime think of you and you just appear. How did your day go?"

Winston concentrated on the part that he most wanted to correct. He had been thinking of her too. "My day went well," he said. "It was this morning I could have done without."

"What...." she sputtered puzzled. "This morning?"

Frustrated he said, "Is it possible that you could find the time to stay longer in the mornings. Why can't I ever find you in bed?"

She laughed with that melodious sound he always enjoyed. "Didn't you get my note?"

"I wanted something other than paper," he said harshly.

"What? You wanted to make love?"

No, that wasn't important, he thought. What he needed was to have her there with him, to talk with, to laugh with, to hold.

"I asked you a question," he said and immediately realized that he must have sounded angry because her smile disappeared.

"Tell me what's really the issue," she said softly.

"I just did. It isn't that difficult a question. Why did you leave?"

"My note told you, but apparently you want to hear something else."

"I want you to promise not to do that again," he said. "Have breakfast with me or something before you go."

"Winston," she said softly as she caressed his cheek. "You've been honest with what you've wanted since the moment we met. But I think you *needed* me...this morning. That's different. And you're upset about it."

"Melanie," he grabbed her and forcefully pulled her to him. "Can you just *be* with me the next time."

"I won't say no if you ask me to, Winston."

"Don't leave me sleeping in the morning," he said. It was a demand and he knew it.

"I won't leave." She tiptoed up and kissed his mouth. "I promise."

He deepened the kiss.

"Go get a room you two!" Sandra said, stopping next to them. "It's downright frustrating for a woman like me to see this stuff and not have a man close by."

"Hi, Sandra." Winston turned to her.

"Hi, yourself," Sandra said. "Papeete in a few hours. You guys planning to get off the ship tonight?"

"I'm going to have a relaxing night on board," Melanie said. "Possibly go to the musical."

"I'm doing what Melanie's doing," Winston added.

Sandra grinned. "You two do that," she said. "I'll find something to do with myself tonight." She turned to leave then stopped. "Mel? Do you still want to meet for breakfast in the morning?"

Melanie smiled up at Winston. "Sure, but let's make it a little later than planned. Say eight instead of seven? Then we'll head to the disembarkation meeting together."

"Don't forget to pack tonight and put the luggage you want to go to the airport outside the room door," Sandra said. "They'll pick it up to be stored to take to the airport."

"I've already packed," Melanie said. "I'm taking my camera, toiletries, a change of clothing and my swimsuit to the hotel. Everything else I can live without until I get to LA."

"Remember to not pack your jacket," Sandra laughed. "So you won't freeze on the plane on the way back this time."

"Oh, you're so funny," Melanie said, smiling.

Sandra turned to Winston. "Are you joining Mel and me on the tour of the city tomorrow?"

"I have a final meeting in Papeete," Winston said, looking back at Melanie, "You have a day room at *Le Meridien* Hotel?" When she said yes, he added, "So do I. I'll meet you both at the hotel for a late lunch. We'll spend some time at the beach or something before heading to the airport."

"I think the plane leaves at 10 p.m.," Sandra added. "So let's do the beach, then I'm napping before we leave."

They said their good-byes and Sandra left. Winston stood beside Melanie as she took pictures of the setting sun.

"That was an incredible sunset," Winston said. "You're going to have to get me prints of those."

"I'll do better than that. I'll enlarge a few of the nicer sunsets I've taken since we've been here."

"Are you always this great?" Winston asked taking a step closer to her. "You make me feel so good, always thinking of things to make me smile. You're wonderful to be with, incredible in bed, and now you give me gifts."

"Am I?" Melanie asked surprised and honing in on the part she most needed to hear.

"Yes, you're great to be with."

"No. Am I really incredible in bed?"

She looked so serious. He took another step and slipped his hands around her waist. "When you're not making love to me, I'm dreaming that you are. Every time has been an adventure with you. I like the sounds you make when you're in my arms." Winston pulled her against him. "I also like how you enjoy exploring your desires with me. Thinking about it is turning me on."

"I guess that means yes," Melanie said, linking her arms around his neck.

"It means that I can't think of anyone else I would rather be with."

Melanie was so pleased she smiled. She could truly please a man. The one thing she thought she would never be able to do. And she pleased him so much that he wished only to be with her.

"You keep this up, Winston, and I'm going to become addicted to you."

"Please do," he said and bent down to kiss her softly.

When he pulled back she said with a smile, "What plans do you have for me tonight?"

"First dinner." He kissed her brow. "Then the show." He kissed the side of her eye. "Then I'm taking you to bed." He kissed her cheek. "We ain't sleeping either."

"Uhhhhh, I like that last part," she said huskily. "Help me with my camera so that we can get started."

The next morning the sunshine warmly kissed the deck of the *Paul Gauguin*. Melanie lay in bed, holding Winston's warmer, nude body. She had been awake for about ten minutes waiting for him to stir. He was sleeping soundly on his back as she lay on her side caressing his chest.

Melanie really wanted to get up and work on putting the finishing touches to her articles. She had completed the drafts for two but wanted to add more facts about the islands to them. Slipping his leg from over hers, she carefully got out of bed, not wanting to wake him. She would at least brush her teeth, she thought.

In the bathroom, Melanie decided to do more. She took a quick shower. Afterwards, she put on vanilla lotion then pulled her hair back into a ponytail. She went and got her purse and put on a touch of lipgloss. Liking the look, she returned to the bedroom. Winston had moved and was resting on his side, his back to her. She found the shirt he had worn last night and slipped it over her nude body. She wanted his spicy, manly smell all around her.

Maybe she would keep this shirt to carry back to Denver with her. Denver, she thought. So, so far away from Winston. Holding him when he woke would be impossible.

It had been troublesome for her to work out a teaching arrangement with the university. Being able to start over in a different city would be very difficult. Her writing was bringing in an income, but not enough to maintain her lifestyle without a supplemental income.

What were they going to do?

And was it worth it? Would it be the same back in the normal world where work and life made it hard on for couples, not even considering the hundreds of miles between them?

She decided to think about this later.

Easing back in bed, she crawled up behind Winston and wrapped an arm around his waist. It was 6:40 a.m. and they needed to start their day. Melanie fit her body close to his and moved her hand down over his soft penis.

"Winston," she whispered in his ear. "I wanted to tell you how good you felt inside me last night...." Then, in provocatively erotic details, she did. Courage came easy when the other person was sleeping. She kissed his ear and nibbled his neck as she recited her tale. As she did, the spell she cast between his legs brought his manhood to life in her hand.

"Winston, I think you want to do it again," she said.

He moved and squirmed as he turned toward her. Opening his eyes he smiled. "Hey," he said before wrapping his arms around her. "You smell good. And what you're doing feels terrific."

He had told her to indulge her fantasies, so she would do just that. "Want a taste?" she asked.

"Of?" he responded.

She moved over him so that her knees were on either side of his waist as she faced his feet. She leaned forward and kissed his stomach, then moved farther down. "Of me," she said, taking his hardness in her hand. "As I taste you."

"Don't ever change, Melanie. I want you just the way you are."

"And I want you just as much," she said, enjoying the sounds he made as she explored his body.

19

The tour of Papeete was more exhausting than expected. It started on Tahiti-nui, the largest of the French Polynesian islands, and ended on Tahiti-iti, the small peninsula connected to Tahiti-nui.

Before leaving on the tour, Melanie and Sandra had breakfast, attended the disembarkation meeting where airline representatives assisted in getting luggage tagged and ticketed, and answering questions. Then they walked across the street to the Internet Café so Melanie could email her article outlines to the magazine editors.

Later they joined a busload of tourists for a seventy-five mile drive around the island, stopping at points of interest for lectures, pictures and shopping, and ending at *Le Meridien* Hotel.

Melanie was grateful. "I need a nap," she said as she stepped off the air-conditioned bus.

"You're supposed to meet Winston for lunch," Sandra reminded her. "You want to rest for an hour or so in the room then go to the restaurant?"

"If I sleep now, I won't get up," Melanie said.

They checked into the room and Melanie decided on a cool shower to shock life back into her.body. Because of the enjoyable late night and early morning romp in bed with Winston, she hadn't gotten much rest.

As she stood in the shower, hands running over her body, it brought back memories of being with him. She was thrilled that he loved her forwardness in bed, and telling her so made her want to please him even more. The surprising part to Melanie was that she didn't feel promiscuous. She had access to a man who wanted to enjoy her just as much as she wanted to enjoy him. It was that simple. And he always seemed to know what she needed from him.

As Melanie came out of the bathroom wrapped in a towel, Sandra asked with a grin, "Is that a hickey on your chest?"

"No," Melanie lied. "And you know we agreed years ago not to give details of our sexual encounters."

"So you admit getting laid!" Sandra practically shouted. "How many times?"

"I'm not participating in this conversation." Melanie stepped into her aqua swimsuit. She reached for a turquoise and gold *pareu* and wrapped it around her waist. "After lunch are we going to the pool or beach?"

"The pool has shade. I'm Black and my tan is just fine the way it is!"

"Put on more sunscreen," Melanie teased, laughing. "But actually I'm more interested in napping after lunch."

"Tell me more about the hickey and stop changing the subject."

"You know the rules. Your business is yours and mine is mine."

"If we had talked more before, you wouldn't have had the problems you had with Ronald. I'm just trying to make sure you're okay with Winston."

"Nothing could have helped with Ronald. He thought he was a great lover. He wasn't. Not by a long shot."

"And Winston?"

"Winston allows me to indulge myself," Melanie said, grinning. "And I'm not saying anything else about our sex life."

"Then I guess we're ready to go to lunch." Sandra stood.

"I'll call Winston and have him meet us," Melanie said.

"Hurry up, I'm hungry." Sandra led the way across the courtyard to the restaurant, which looked out over the pool and beach beyond.

"What are you and Winston going to do when we get back to the U.S. of loving A?" Sandra asked at the table. They had ordered tea as they waited for him.

"We haven't decided," Melanie admitted. "I want this with him, Sandra. But I don't know how to swing losing half my income to move to Dallas. And I know he won't give up his practice there. It's his life and I won't ask him to."

"I can tell by the way you two respond to each other that this is more than a hot fling. I'm completely jealous."

"You can have any man you want," Melanie said, "You don't want a serious relationship."

"That's not what I'm jealous of! I didn't get laid not one time the whole damn cruise," Sandra whispered, embarrassed at having to admit that. "Now it's over!"

"What?" Melanie started to laugh. "You had plenty of opportunity!"

"I was so busy reviewing all of them that I never got around to selecting one. Besides, most didn't seem honest enough to make me comfortable with them. Last night I tried to make a date with my doctor friend and he gave me the brush off. Free stuff and he turned it down!"

"You had probably turned him down all week," Melanie said. "Turnabout is fair play!"

"Let's change the subject," Sandra replied. "I might cry if I think of all the fun times I've missed. Let's go back to talking about Winston."

"My favorite topic."

"I have an idea." Sandra was suddenly serious. "Don't say anything. Just think about it for a while."

"Okay."

"You know I have a three-bedroom home," Sandra offered up. "Stay with me until you decide if you want to be with Winston long term. You can take your time looking for a job in Dallas."

"I have my life, my job, my future in Denver. I just can't up and move on the hopes of a relation...."

Sandra interrupted. "I said think about it first! Don't talk it through now or you'll talk yourself out of it before even really considering it."

"We're different types of people, Sandra. I love you to death, but I'm a workaholic and you're a party girl. I don't think our differences will let us live together."

"We were roommates in college," Sandra reminded her. "We can do it again. I'll continue to party, and you'll do what you do."

"I don't know if...." Melanie started, but Sandra interrupted again.

"Just think about it, Girl!"

"Okay, I'll think about it." Melanie laughed.

Absorbed in their own thoughts they were both quiet for a moment.

Melanie suddenly asked, "Remember what I said in the airport after seeing Winston?"

Sandra reflected. "Yes, I do."

"I think it's coming true," Melanie almost whispered, looking out over the pool.

"That's reason enough right there to move to Dallas."

As Winston headed to the door, his telephone rang. "Melanie, again." He smiled as he picked up the telephone, "You can't wait to see me, right? Is that why you called?"

"Yes it is! I've missed you, Sweetheart. Since I couldn't reach you on the ship, I called the hotel."

"Daphne?" Winston drew a deep breath and exhaled slowly. "I guess you do have my itinerary."

"How was the cruise?" Daphne asked.

"Better than I could have imagined."

"Even without me?" she pouted, and Winston knew she was poking out her bottom lip.

"I'm headed out, Daphne," he said, wanting to end this conversation. Listening to her pout wasn't something he wanted to do at the end of this wonderful cruise, or ever again for that matter. "I have a lunch date."

"Okay. I just wanted to make sure we were still going to see each other as soon as you get back."

"I haven't changed my mind, Daphne," Winston said flatly.

"I'm calling internationally," Daphne answered hurriedly. "You said we'd talk when you got back! I'll wait until then. We have a lot to talk about. Have a safe trip home."

Before Winston could say there was nothing to talk about, Daphne hung up the telephone with a sharp click. Mentally he shook off the dread. Ridding himself of her was taking a lot more effort than he thought it would. Daphne was a pretty woman, a model, but none of that beauty was on the inside. He had discovered a little too late that she wanted the financial security and status of being a doctor's wife.

She had said all the right things in the beginning, feeding on his loneliness. But when she started giving him her bills to pay and their dates consisted of his taking her shopping at exclusive stores, he realized she wasn't all she made herself out to be. Her smile was too fake, her laugh too brittle, and her desire to be with him had nothing to do with enjoying him, and everything to do with what she could get out of him.

Then he thought of Melanie. She was just the opposite. She made him feel wanted and cared only about making him smile. Her laugh was so real. She was so real. Suddenly he felt a terrible need to be with her right now. He turned and hurried out.

He saw Melanie, sitting with Sandra at a table in the restaurant. The ocean backdrop behind them added a calming element to the view. It helped him to rid himself of thoughts of Daphne.

When he approached the table, Melanie turned and extended a hand to him. "Hey, Sweetie!"

"Hey, Baby," Winston said, bending to kiss her as he held her hand. "Did you have fun today?"

"Much. But I missed having you with me. It would have been a lot more fun with you."

"Just what I needed to hear." Winston kissed her again, this time longer.

"Enough with the lovey-dovey stuff," Sandra teased.

Winston laughed and reached for his chair.

"No kiss for me?" Sandra whined and he went over and gave her a smack on the cheek. "That's better."

"We were just talking about you," Melanie said as he sat down.

"How so?"

"We went to the Gauguin Museum. I saw a print of the piece you were interested in. If I'd known the area you wanted to decorate, I would have gotten it for you."

Winston looked at her for long moments. Again she just wanted to please him. "We have time to go back. Come with me when I do?"

"I would love to. How did the meeting go?"

"Just like the rest of them," he answered. "I would have preferred touring the city with you two."

"It was exhausting," Melanie said, "but fun. Especially the museums. I like learning all about Gauguin: his wife, his mistresses, the bouts with syphilis and depression, the fights with the church, his mistresses and his countrymen."

Sandra added. "He seemed angry at himself and the world. I don't see any of that in his art. Only the peacefulness of the islands."

"That's why I'm interested in a few prints," Winston added before standing and pulling Melanie out of the chair. He wrapped his arm around her. "Come on, Sandra. Let's get lunch. And then let's head to the museum."

Flight TN2 to Los Angeles was leaving on time.

The three had met Chuck at the hotel, and they all rode to the airport together. The check-in was uneventful and everyone was aboard, ready for takeoff. Melanie sat at the window with Winston next to her on the aisle.

Sitting on the aisle opposite Winston, Chuck said, "This trip was worth every penny."

"I second that," Sandra added, seated next to him.

Winston turned to Melanie. "Are you going to keep me company or sleep this time?"

"I'll chat with you for a while. And I'll be here in the morning when you wake."

He laughed. "I like doing mornings with you, especially this morning."

"Winston, after tomorrow, when will we spend another morning together?"

He looked at her, his face serious. This was one of many times today that he had thought that same thing. "I'm planning to come to Colorado as soon as I can. I'll be in LA for a week visiting my sister. I want to see you next weekend."

"That's a great idea," Melanie agreed.

As the plane took off, Winston turned to her. "I won't let you forget me. I need you in my life." He planted a kiss on her forehead. "Something very special started on that ship. I can't let you walk away. I want you, Melanie McDae."

"I want you, too." She placed her hand on his and squeezed. "A lot."

A week ago, he had stood in the airport certain that this trip would be just another temporary fix of joy, like taking a pain pill for a permanent illness. Now he had his cure. But it hadn't happened until he had loosened his grip on his career and reached out for something more than work, something that would bring the happiness he sought. Work wasn't what he needed, not at all. He needed someone to care for him, to love him.

At first, it had been Melanie's laugh that called to him, her smile that beckoned him. Now it was her spirit, her kindness, her sensuality, her honesty and openness. He would be damned before he eased his grip on his chance for happiness with her. No matter the distance.

Those pleasant thoughts were on his mind as he drifted off to sleep.

As the night turned into morning, the captain of Flight TN2 informed the passengers that they would be in California in less than two hours.

Winston awoke dreaming of Melanie. Another morning without emptiness, he thought happily. The closer you floated to heaven surely the easier it was for prayers to be heard.

"Good morning," Melanie said.

"Yes, it is," Winston agreed.

After the plane landed in the U.S., they headed down the corridor to check the bus to the terminal for customs. The check-in for returning U.S. citizens was much faster, but getting luggage out of customs was a joke.

"Do you think our luggage made it back into the country?" Sandra asked, sitting on the floor, her back against the wall. "It's been thirty minutes." She looked at the empty luggage conveyor belt.

"Another few minutes," Chuck said, as he plopped next to her.

"You've said that the last eight times I asked you," Sandra complained. "They've probably got dogs sniffing stuff for contraband. Luckily, we can recheck it down here and not have to carry those heavy suitcases up to the terminal."

"That's the good part," Chuck laughed.

"You know, Chuck," Sandra said, looking at Winston and Melanie leaning arm-in-arm against the wall. "I take full credit for those two unmarried newlyweds getting together."

Chuck laughed. "Melanie never did correct that little misunderstanding did she?"

Sandra laughed, too. "I don't think Winston really minds."

The conveyor belt finally started and the passengers clapped and cheered. Everyone began collecting their luggage and heading in different directions.

Since the connecting flights weren't leaving for another few hours, Winston, Melanie, Sandra and Chuck planned to have breakfast together at the airport.

As they exited the international gates, Chuck stopped and cursed. "Oh, shit!" he said distressed and looking around. "Where's Winston!"

"What?" Sandra asked after seeing the alarmed look on his face. "What's wrong?"

"We have trouble." Chuck hurried toward Winston, who was coming up from behind, holding Melanie's hand. "It's his lady friend."

"Whose?" Sandra yelled running to keep up with Chuck, her large bag flopping across her shoulder.

"Winston's!"

"That bastard!" Sandra rushed around Chuck, heading for Melanie. "I've got to get Melanie out of this!"

"It's not what you think," Chuck said. He waved to get Winston's attention, then pointed toward Daphne.

"Daphne?" Winston said. "What is she doing here?"

"Who are you talking about?" Melanie said, concerned after seeing his face. Then she saw Sandra rushing toward them.

"How the hell could you do this to Melanie?" Sandra shouted at Winston.

"Winston," Chuck said stopping next to them. "She's here."

"Who's here," Melanie asked.

"Winston's girlfriend," Sandra said angrily.

"Daphne," Chuck blurted out.

Winston winced at the shocking surprise on Melanie's face.

"Winston!" Daphne called. She rushed up to the group and said cheerfully, "Baby doll, welcome back!"

Melanie took in the tall, slender, pretty woman in front of them. She was pecan tan with long, flowing hair. Even at this time of morning, she had on makeup and was impeccably dressed in a cream sundress with pearls. Her smile turned to an exaggerated frown when she realized Melanie was holding Winston's hand.

"Winston?" Melanie barely whispered.

"Who the hell are you?" Daphne snapped, one French-manicured nail pointing at Melanie.

"What are you doing here?" Winston said to Daphne.

Daphne ignored the question. "So this is why you didn't want me in Tahiti!" Her anger bubbling. "You were taking your trip tramp?"

Tramp! Sandra took exception to that insult. "Bitch, you don't know us well enough to call names!" She snatched her bag off her shoulder as she went toward Daphne.

Chuck jumped between them. "Don't do this, Sandra."

"She started it!" Sandra allowed Chuck to refrain her by the shoulders.

"Daphne is your girlfriend?" Melanie asked Winston.

"Yes I am," Daphne answered. "And I don't appreciate you disrespecting me like this, Winston!"

"Daphne, you're mistaken again," Winston snapped. "And I asked you what the hell you're doing here."

"Chuck, take you hands off me!" Sandra's anger was about to explode. "Melanie, let's get out of here."

"You said we would talk when you got back," Daphne corrected Winston.

"Daphne!" Chuck demanded. "What are you doing here. Why?"

Four sets of eyes all registered shock when Daphne finally responded.

"I came because of the baby!" Daphne screamed. "Because of the baby!" she repeated, clearly on the verge of tears.

Everyone went silent, still.

Melanie's eyes dropped to Daphne's stomach. She noticed the puffy roundness on an otherwise slimmer body.

"Winston," Melanie couldn't keep the hurt out of her voice, "You call this being honest with me? You said there was no one of consequence in your life. Excuse me." She turned and walked off as Sandra hurried to catch up with her.

"Melanie, wait!" Winston called after her.

"Winston, we need to talk!" Daphne shouted, reaching for his hand.

Melanie stopped, turned, and in a voice choking with despair said, "Don't ever speak to me again." Sandra took her arm to lead her away. "We were a mistake."

20

If there was ever a moment that Melanie most wanted to forget. This was it.

"Melanie, slow down!" Sandra shouted, running to catch up. "Stop!"

"Leave me alone, Sandra!" Melanie yelled over her shoulder. "If you had stayed out of my business with Winston, this wouldn't have happened."

"Melanie!" Sandra reached for her arm, halting her. "I said stop!"

"You don't want a piece of me right now," Melanie snatched her arm away and continued hurrying down the airport's corridor.

"You don't think this is hurting me, too?" Sandra said, walking fast next to her. "This is all my fault!"

That stopped Melanie in her tracks. Everyone could claim blame. She looked and saw tears in Sandra's eyes. Then she pointed a finger at Sandra's chest. "Don't you dare cry! We will not talk about this now and you will not cry for me!" She felt tears swell in her own eyes. "I will not allow Winston to hurt me!"

"Mel," Sandra said softly, tears leaking. "He already has."

Melanie started walking again, then she started to run. She ran past groups of travelers, various shops, down the escalator, around corners and halls until she was outside. The sun was terribly bright, the air cool.

But he hadn't seen any of it because it all was a wet, miserable blur. Gulping for breath, she leaned against a wall. It hurt to breathe; it hurt not too. But mostly it hurt to think of the fool she had been. How could she have trusted him with her heart?

How did she allow herself to be hurt again? *Not again, God. Please, not again.*

Then she burst into tears. She wasn't even remotely embarrassed about the sad condition she was in as people passed, some even staring. Finally, she wiped her tears, lifted her chin and headed back into the airport terminal.

She saw Sandra sitting in a chair, waiting for her. Sandra stood, walked to close the distance.

"Can I treat you to a cup of coffee?" Sandra asked.

"Can I have a hug first?" Melanie answered. She got one, then they headed back outside where they flagged a cab. "Let's take a later flight out. I don't feel like being here right now. I need a quiet place to think."

The coffee did little for Melanie's sinking spirits, but Sandra's warm friendship had helped. They talked about everything except what had happened at the airport.

They had been friends long enough for Sandra to know that Melanie needed to internalize her thoughts before she could talk about them. She had always handled difficult situations that way. It allowed her to review the situation and come up with sound options.

"Look what I got," Sandra said, pulling out chocolate covered coconut candies. "I picked them up in the airport before we left Tahiti."

"Just what I need." Melanie reached for a piece.

"I charged my phone on the ship before we left," Sandra reached in her purse. "Let's call the airlines and schedule something out for a few days from now. We can drive to Disneyland from here and play for a couple of days."

"I thought you planned to return to work Monday?"

"I'd rather play than work," Sandra said. "I'll call information to get a number for our airlines."

"There's probably a number on our itinerary," Melanie said, reaching into her bag, noticing her own hand trembling, paused forgetting about the document. "You don't have to give up more vacation time to nurse me. I'll be okay in a little while."

"Are you sure?"

"Yeah," Melanie said as more tears trickled from her eyes. "I'm fine."

"I don't think so. But I'm hear to talk when you're ready."

Melanie busied herself with searching for the itinerary. "I just need time to think this over by myself first."

"You don't have a 9-to-5 to rush back to. Come home with me and hang out for awhile. When you're ready to talk, I'll be just a room away."

"I don't know." Melanie reached for a napkin to wipe her tears. "I really need to get back to Denver."

"No you don't," Sandra corrected.

The waitress showed up. "More coffee?"

"Sure," Melanie passed her cup and was thankful for the interruption. She was on the verge of crying again. It wasn't like her to weep this much.

Sandra picked up the breakfast menu. "I'll have pancakes and sausage also. Anything, Mel?"

"Bring me the same," Melanie said. She wasn't hungry, but she wanted to have something else to focus on.

When Sandra checked with the airlines, she learned all direct flights to Denver were sold out, but connecting flights were available.

"Melanie, you have a choice of connecting flights through Dallas or Arizona."

"If I can, I'll fly with you to Dallas," Melanie said. "Then continue on the Denver. What time will I get home?"

Sandra asked the reservationist, then said, "Either way, you'll get home extremely late. Why don't you stay over in Dallas and go home tomorrow morning?"

"Fine."

Sandra made the arrangements.

"Here's my baggage claim ticket," Melanie said. "See if you can get my luggage pulled off the original flight. I would prefer to have it with me than to arrive in Denver tonight."

Breakfast was served and they talked about everything except the Winston ordeal. After breakfast, they sat sipping coffee and waited for the time to catch their flight at the restaurant instead of the airport.

They talked very little on the flight to Dallas. Melanie either read a novel or reviewed her research notes for her articles. It was a means of escape. She needed to put Winston out of her thoughts, and concentrating on work helped.

She had cared for a deceitful man most of her adult life and thought she had gotten good at reading signs of disloyalty and deception. But since she had missed such signs with Winston, she concluded that she had more to learn. Winston had been so convincing.

Or maybe she had been so desperate for someone to nourish her heart that she overlooked clues that would have prevented this.

Winston had a girlfriend. No, Melanie thought. Winston had a *pregnant* girlfriend. One who had been expecting to meet him upon his return to Los Angeles. She probably wanted to plan the baby's christening.

Stop it Melanie, she scolded herself. *You were played and used. Accept it and move on.*

Melanie exhaled a ragged breath. She was tired. The air travel that started last night had gotten the best of her. Since she was breaking this trip home into parts by staying a night with Sandra, she would have time to try to get a full night's rest. Besides, waking up alone tomorrow to an empty house was something she wanted to avoid.

She had no reason to rush home—no classes to teach, no pet to feed. The airlines had managed to stop her luggage from going to Denver, so she could actually stay in Dallas a few days, or a week for that matter, and finish her articles before returning home.

"Sandra?" When Melanie turned to her, she put down the magazine. "I'm thinking of staying a few days in Dallas. Would that be okay with you?"

"Of course," Sandra attempted a weak smile. "I've already asked if you would. Remember?" When Melanie nodded she added, "I can take off Monday and we can play in Dallas."

"Let's decide on that later," Melanie said. "I'm planning to work while I'm there."

"Work?" Sandra questioned in disbelief.

"It will help me, Sandra. And I'll have you there if I decide to play some."

"Okay! I'm glad you're staying."

Melanie took a deep breath then closed her eyes. Although she tried to stop it from happening, images of her times with Winston filled her mind, making her heart ache more. It would be difficult, but she would figure out a way to forget about him.

She had to....

21

There really was a baby.

Daphne had not lied about that, but she had also twisted the situation to her advantage, Winston realized much too late. Before he discovered the details, he had left Daphne to find Melanie.

When he momentarily turned to calm Daphne, Melanie had disappeared in the crowd. He ran down the corridor to find her, but she was gone. Then he checked the gate of the last direct flight to Denver, but she wasn't there.

When he had returned to claim his carry-on bag from Chuck, Daphne was gone, leaving a message for him to call her cellular or meet her at his sister Ashley's, house.

Instead, Winston went with Chuck, hoping Melanie was on that flight with Sandra. Neither had been there.

He stood watching the departure of Chuck's plane half-hoping Sandra and Melanie would show up late. They didn't. He turned to leave.

He needed to handle this unexpected baby surprise. But first he would rent a car, possibly call Daphne and have her meet him some place other than his sister's house. He had expected Ashley and her husband, Greg, to pick him up. Since they hadn't been there, Winston concluded Daphne had something to do with that. He reached for his cellular phone and realized he had forgotten to recharge it. Calling her would have to wait.

He would hurry to his sister's and deal with Daphne. If she were there, crying on Ashley's shoulder, this could get pretty messy.

Winston should have told his sister to strike Daphne from her invitation list. Although she was originally included, once Winston had ended the affair and cancelled her trip to Tahiti, it should have been clear to her that the invitation was cancelled. But he knew Daphne, and being specific was a requirement with her, or she would use the vagueness to her advantage.

Why else would Daphne fly all the way from Dallas? Unless the pregnancy and reuniting were something she wanted to discuss immediately, possibly using his sister to help support her cause. He'd wanted to be a father one day, but not like this...Not with Daphne.

Damn!

He had taken precautions to prevent things like this, but nature sometimes had its way regardless. And being a doctor, he had seen many unplanned pregnancies that changed lives forever.

Damn! Damn!

As Winston reached the driveway of his sister's home, he was relieved to see no other cars. Maybe Daphne hadn't arrived yet, so he would get to enjoy a little time with Ashley before dealing with the pregnancy issue. It would definitely be dealt with today. Just later.

Luck wasn't on his side, so he prayed nothing else would happen with Daphne that could ruin his sister's party plans for tonight. She'd been planning it for weeks. Winston really wanted to hop on a plane to Denver, but felt obliged to be there, although now he wasn't in a partying mood.

Ashley said it would be just a cozy get-together with friends and family, but her parties always blossomed into a celebration of many sorts.

He would be there for his sister even though he didn't want to be. She had planned the event around his visit and he didn't want to hurt her feelings too. He couldn't hurt another woman today.

Getting out of the car, Winston felt like one had just hit him. Inhaling strength, he mentally shook himself then headed to the front door. By the time he reached it, Ashley had opened it.

"Winston!" she yelled, leaping into his arms. "I'm so glad to see you!"

"Hey, Lil Sis! You're looking great." he hugged her tight, allowing his problems to fade for the moment. "Where's Greg?"

"He's out running last minute errands for tonight's party. He swears no one can out cook him." When Winston stepped inside the house, she stood looking outside. "Where's Daphne?"

"I'm not sure," Winston said vaguely. He wasn't certain of how to broach the conversation. Obviously, Daphne must have called ahead.

"But I thought she was picking you up at the airport?"

"She wasn't there when I left." Winston didn't want to relive the airport ordeal just yet. Then he frowned. One moment with Daphne and he was already back to half-truths and partial statements. Melanie had immediately picked up on the habit that had become a norm with him—a defense mechanism to appease Daphne's delicate feelings. She didn't like dealing directly with issues, so he found himself telling her what she needed to hear to keep the peace. Yet Melanie had refused to deal with him when he did such things and accused him of manipulating the conversation and misleading her. What had become an acquired art form for dealing with Daphne was now an annoyance. He liked being able to express himself honestly to the woman in his life.

Ashley interrupted his thoughts. "I hope she isn't lost. I was too sick this morning to make it out, so Daphne went by herself. I thought she would be able to find the airport since she drove herself from it last night," Ashley said walking passed Winston to get to the family room. "I still don't understand why she would blow off a trip to Tahiti, but would want to come to LA for a rib sandwich. Anyway, I set up the second bedroom for you two."

Ashley was full of surprising news. First, was the remark that she was sick. Next, was the revelation that Daphne has pulled an unannounced visit to her house last night. If only he had told his sister about the breakup, but Winston concentrated on the immediate issue.

"You're not feeling well?" He came to stand next to her.

"Morning sickness...Didn't you...What am I thinking about? You haven't spoken to Daphne yet, so you don't know about my surprise!" Ashley glowed with delight. "I'm finally pregnant!" she yelled.

It took Winston a few moments to digest that. "So *you're* pregnant?" he said dumbfounded.

"Yes!" Ashley admitted. was planning to make the grand announcement tonight at the party. But surprise!"

Winston again hugged his sister. "At least I can be happy for you."

"You know I've been trying for two years, Winston! If we hadn't made this baby I would have adopted."

"Yeah. I know."

Ashley stepped back. "Don't sound so glum! I'm floating on a cloud! So be happy with me!"

Winston was becoming overwhelmed by the constant change of events that had started after stepping off the plane. But he mustered up a little joy. "I am."

"Good! Now you need to marry, so that you can give my baby a cousin!" Ashley was almost bouncing when she said that, but Winston's face fell. Joy disappeared.

"It seems I'm going to be able to give you that very soon."

"Stop joking." His sister turned, heading down the hall. "You said you'd never have a baby out of wedlock. And since you're not married..."

He interrupted. "I think Daphne is pregnant."

Ashley froze, then turned to face him. "She never said a thing, even when I told her about my morning sickness. My party is going to be great! We both have something to celebrate tonight!"

He needed to squelch her excitement, even though it hurt to do so. "I'm afraid not. My relationship with Daphne has been over for months. This isn't how I wanted to be a father."

22

"Daphne had mentioned a pregnancy at the airport. God! Maybe she wasn't talking about herself, but you. Things got out of hand so fast, I'm not sure now exactly what she said."

Ashley sat down on the sofa in the living room next to him. "Wait a minute, so you did see Daphne at the airport? I'm confused."

"It's a long, unpleasant story that I don't have time to get into right now," Winston said as he paced the floor. "I really need to talk to Daphne and figure out what the hell is going on. It's over with her, and I definitely don't plan to rekindle that relationship."

"Then what are you going to do if she's pregnant?"

Winston shook his head. "I was so careful to prevent this from happening."

"And you're sure she is?"

He reflected on the airport incident. *He, like everyone one else, had glared at Daphne's stomach. It was slightly larger than normal. Perfectly distended. She looked pregnant, but maybe it was his imagination. Maybe it* was *his sister Daphne had been talking about. It made sense didn't it? Ashley was suffering from morning sickness, so Daphne had come in her place?* "I'm not sure of anything," he groaned.

"For her to pull this unannounced visit, something must be up," Ashley concluded. "Why else would she show up here in L.A. knowing the relationship is over?"

"She called me in Tahiti. Now this visit. She's up to something." He rubbed a frustrated hand across his head. "This is why I ended that relationship. Too much stress. Too much drama."

"I'm not one of those sisters who sticks her nose into other people's relationships, but I never thought Daphne was right for you. If she is pregnant with your baby, what will you do?"

"Let's take this one step at a time." Winston picked up the telephone. "That scene Daphne made at the airport was to cause problems between me and Melanie. I just need to know to what extent she has gone."

"Melanie?"

"You'll like her, Ash. I certainly do. I met her on the cruise and there's something very special about her."

"I know I like the way you smile when you talk about her. This is the first genuine smile you've had since getting here."

"That's the part I also like." Winston dialed the number he'd wanted to erase from memory.

Daphne answered her cellular on the second ring. When he discovered she was at a mall closer to the airport than to his sister's, he made arrangements to meet her there for lunch.

"I'm going up to pack her things," Winston said after hanging up. "I'm not particularly interested in Daphne living here, causing static with the family."

"Will she be a problem?" Ashley stood, concerned. "Because I'm not so pregnant that I can't correct her if I need to. This is my house and we're celebrating your visit and my baby. I won't let her ruin it regardless of her condition."

"Don't worry, Ash," His sister's sassiness always made him grin. "Daphne's no fool, but I've got to go deal with this."

"Go handle your business. I'll butt out of it for the time being."

Driving to the restaurant, Winston replayed the last time he'd had sex with Daphne. She had been overly eager, almost demanding it. He knew enough about a woman's physiology to know she'd been ovulating. That was why he made sure, particularly sure that time, to have extra condoms. She'd complained that he was ruining the mood by stopping to put one on, but he had anyway.

That was four months ago. Long enough for Daphne to show. He hoped it was weight gain, but the moment he spotted her in the restaurant, he knew the truth.

Let her be less than four months, he prayed. A reason to question the fatherhood.

"It seems you and my sister are both pregnant." Winston slid into the restaurant's booth. Luckily it was in the back, had some privacy.

"Isn't that wonderful! She's always wanted a baby. You always talked about having a family. Now you both will be starting a family at the same time."

Winston's stomach turned.

"But I didn't want you to find out like this, Sweetheart." Daphne looked completely at peace, glowing.

"Yes you did. You accomplished just what you hoped to at the airport. You caused problems."

"I can't believe you said that!" Daphne's big, brown eyes watered quickly. She reached for a napkin and dabbed at them trying to squeeze out tears. "I'm so emotional now that I'm pregnant."

He ignored the strained tears. She always cried to get her way. "How far along are you?"

"Almost five months."

Damn! It could be mine! Disappointment was starting to twist his insides.

"I wasn't going to tell you at all." She dabbed some more. "But I can't raise this baby by myself. I couldn't keep your baby from you like that. That would be so wrong. When I called you in Tahiti and you said there was a chance for us, I immediately got on a plane. I had to come back to you. Try and make it work for our baby's sake. I want our child to be raised knowing his father, carrying the Knight's name."

Lord no! Winston knew if he ate something it would probably come back up. He cherished kids. Wanted his own. But marrying a woman he'd loathed for months wasn't what he had planned. Neither was raising a child by her. But he would never turn his back on his own. Winston realized his palms were sweaty and he rubbed them forcefully down the fronts of his jeans.

His happiness couldn't end like this. Not like this. There had to be another answer. He blinked a few times hoping to wash away the nightmare.

"Want breakfast?" Daphne asked sweetly, intruding into his thoughts.

Winston ignored her question, reaching for hope, "You were seeing someone else during that same time. How can you be sure if it's mine?"

An ugly scowl marred Daphne's pretty face. "Why would you say something that disgusting to me!" The scowl changed to shock. "This is because of that woman at the airport? You're with someone else, therefore I must have been with someone else!" She was whimpering now. Real tears formed. "You never mentioned her before. Why all of a sudden does she matter? Why all of a sudden I don't matter!"

In the past, Winston would have backed off at moments like this. Daphne knew it. They both did. It was how things had worked best between them. She made demands and continued to push with emotional tears then he would try to appease.

But now, his own shock, anger and needs came to the forefront. "All you need to know is that she does matter. More than you'll ever understand. She's the kind of woman I've been needing in my life, which is why there can never be an "us" again, Daphne."

"So you were cheating on me! You admit it! Is that why you decided to take her on this trip in my place? One week with her and you're throwing all that we had away? Turning your back on me when I need you…"

"Calm down," Winston snapped. Things were getting out of control. The next step for Daphne would be to stand, cry, and make a scene he didn't want to deal with. "You never answered my question!" he said sternly, forcing her to quiet down. "Why are you convinced it's my child?" Winston knew he shouldn't, wouldn't deny his own child, but he needed hope on his side.

"It's called making love," she said more calmly. "Or have you've forgotten everything we shared?"

Just a little hope. Please. "It's also called using protection when you do. We always had." For a moment, Winston got the impression she was actually reexamining the facts, their history, intimate moments. She had never told him she'd been dating someone else. But he had suspected that she had. Then he saw a shadow of doubt cross her face and quickly vanish. The door was open for his next statement. "And you didn't with the other guy, did you?" He was guessing at that, but he needed to know just how much Daphne was attempting to play him, use this poor baby to win him back. A desperate move, but one that couldn't be overlooked.

"I'm in love with you," she said helplessly, avoiding his stare.

Her lack of denial that there had been other men should have been a stab to his heart. But instead of hurt it felt more like relief. Hope!

Winston had to drive home his point to remove all doubt of amends with her. "I'm not interested in fathering a child from you. We have other options."

Daphne reached down and hugged her stomach as if gripping a small, injured child in her loving arms. "Kill my baby!" She sneered loudly, catching the attention of the people near by. "Is that what you're telling me to do?"

"What I want you to understand is that I've moved on. I'm seeing someone else. The baby will not change that. And before I'd consider raising the child you're carrying, I'll demand proof it's mine. I don't think it is, especially since I'm not sure if you're even five months pregnant."

Gone was the weak, defenseless woman in need. Daphne's fury erupted and she spit out like venom. "You slimy bastard! How could I ever think I wanted you to raise my child! You were never that good in bed in the first place! That's the reason I slept with someone else...He's the father and I..." Her anger was her downfall.

Winston was sure she didn't mean to reveal so much, but he took that as the luck it was. "That's all I needed to hear." Winston stood up and she realized a second too late what she'd just admitted. "We're done, Daphne. Stay away from me. I mean it."

He stormed out, leaving her ranting. The scene should have embarrassed him, but all he felt was relief.

Luckily, hope had been floating over him in that restaurant. In the back of his mind he'd already started a plan to raise the child, if his. But in his heart, he just wanted to escape the ordeal and was given a chance because he refused to back down against Daphne's antics. Outside he inhaled freedom.

He couldn't believe his morning. What should have ended as the best trip of his life went to hell in the blink of an eye because he had given Daphne a chance at reuniting. Now he needed to find Melanie. If only he had told her something about Daphne, her response might not have been so extreme. He would find her, talk to her.

On the return trip to his sister's, Winston mentally brushed off the final remnants of meeting with Daphne. His cellular was recharged, and he immediately called information to get the number of Melanie McDae in the Denver area.

"Damn," he whispered to himself. "No listing." He tried information again, giving names of surrounding cities but couldn't get a number for her. He cursed again for not getting her address and telephone number earlier—a thirty-second exchange that could have happened at any time during the trip, and definitely would have if not for Daphne.

Melanie had his business card, but because of what had happened he knew she would never call him. Winston looked at his watch. It was too soon for Chuck or Sandra to have reached Dallas. They could help with Melanie's contact information, but the best he could do was wait.

"Winston?" Ashley said, opening her front door again. "You don't look so good. What happened with Daphne?"

"Daphne's on her way home," Winston said. "She finally admitted it wasn't my child when I suggested a paternity test."

"How could she come here expecting you wouldn't ask?" Ashley asked in disbelief.

"You've just gotten a sample of what I've gone through with her. Lord, Melanie is a breath of fresh air in comparison. I really need to find her and explain. She still believes Daphne is pregnant with my baby."

"Go call Melanie. Don't let me hold you up."

"I'm having a problem reaching her. I might cut my visit with you short to go to Denver. Maybe leave tomorrow or the day after if that's okay?"

"Stay long enough to help me celebrate my baby, then do what you need to do." Ashley patted his arm.

"The only thing I can do now is wait for Chuck to get home," Winston said. "I don't have Melanie's home phone, if you can belief that. But Chuck has her best friend's number."

"Come on back to the family room," Ashley said. "Let's talk. I'm too much in the dark to be able to help you."

Winston gave Ashley the highlights of meeting Melanie, the wonderful cruise because of her, Daphne's appearance at the airport and the following confusion.

"You sound serious about her," Ashley said.

"I am," Winston agreed. "And it's going to be at least several more hours before I can reach her."

"I would love to meet the woman who's got you so worked up. She must be great."

"I'm going to find her!" Winston promised. "You'll get to meet her soon enough."

"The party will help take your mind off things, until you can talk to Melanie," Ashley comforted. "Why don't you help me set up the patio in the meantime?"

It was an unbearable wait. The party provided only marginal joy for Winston. It had been six hours and still he hadn't received a return call from Chuck.

The sooner he talked to Melanie the better he would feel. And most definitely, the better Melanie would feel. She was probably punishing herself or regretting their experience on the ship. He needed to correct that.

Then his cellular phone rang. It was Chuck.

"Glad you got my message, Chuck". He gave him the highlights of the misunderstanding in the airport and how he had dealt with Daphne before asking, "Do you know how to get in touch with Sandra?"

"Actually, I don't. I don't remember her last name either. She spent some time with Marcus Lowell and his friend, Ralph. Sandra has my business card. If I hear from her, I'll let her know what's going on."

"Thanks, Chuck," Winston said disappointed. "I have Marcus's number. I'll try him."

"Good luck finding her," Chuck said before hanging up.

Luck had brought Melanie into his life; losing her was not something he would let happen—could allow to happen. He got up and went to get Marcus's telephone number.

After a few pleasantries, Winston learned that Marcus had no way of contacting Sandra either, but at least he had her last name. For her to have been such a flirt, she surely was cautious about giving out her number. Calling information, Winston quickly discovered that her number wasn't listed either.

This had become entirely too frustrating, and that angered him. He would lose Melanie if things didn't turn around soon.

"Winston?" Ashley said softly walking into the den. "Any luck?"

"I'm going to lose her, Ash." Winston looked miserable.

"What did she say?"

"Nothing yet." Winston stood up. "I haven't found a way to get in touch with her."

Ashley rounded the desk and stood next to him. She bent down and logged on to the computer sitting on the desk. "Let's see if we can find her on the Internet."

Winston found himself smiling. "Did I ever tell you that you're quite resourceful?"

"Blame Dad."

23

It had been almost a week.

Melanie couldn't find a reason to go home and Sandra didn't want her to leave. They had spent a lot of time touring Dallas and the surrounding cities. They sampled many great restaurants in Addison, TX, ventured to Negro Cowboy events in Mesquite, TX, toured the Ballpark in Arlington, home of baseball's Texas Rangers and went clubbing around Dallas. Melanie wasn't sure what the cure for her broken heart was. Sandra had kept her busy, trying every way she could think of to distract her from misery.

Nothing was working, and Melanie really didn't know what to do.

"Mel, what're your plans for this evening?" Sandra asked entering her spacious family room. The bay window overlooked a sizable yard where her spring flowers were in bloom. Melanie sat sipping coffee and staring at the array of multiple colored flowers.

"I'm waiting on a call about the articles. Based on the feedback I get, I'll probably have to change a few things. So, I might be working this evening. Why?"

"It's Friday night. Don't you want to go dancing instead? Maybe meet for drinks after I get off work then head to a club or something?" Sandra asked.

"We did that last night." Melanie turned back to the patio view. "I'll skip the club hopping tonight."

Sandra walked around the sofa and sat next to her. She reached into her labcoat pocket and pulled out something. "I found Winston's business card in the bathroom trash this morning."

"I put it there," Melanie said.

"I figured that much out myself. It's been a week and you haven't even tried to contact him. Is there a reason why you're taking this lying down? You haven't vented, shouted or anything. Shout, Girl, at *him*," Sandra pleaded. "Get this out of your system."

"I don't feel like shouting," Melanie answered flatly.

"Don't get me wrong," Sandra said. "I love that you're here, and we both know you don't want to be home alone to deal with this. But you're not talking to me about it either. Now his card is in the trash. The least you should do is call and give him a piece of your mind. If you had slapped Winston's face, you might have gotten some of this out of your system."

"Have you ever been slapped, Sandra?"

"Hell, no," Sandra said.

"I have," Melanie said. "Lots of times, by Ronald, and it didn't change my outlook toward him. So why would it change a man who had manipulated the both of us so he could have a fling at my expense? He lost nothing and got everything out of the deal."

"Then confront him so he'll think twice before doing it again. You can protect the next woman," Sandra said. "Then you can vent and bounce back. I've never known you to take this long to bounce back."

"I'm bouncing, Sandra. Just not as fast as you'd like."

"I think you're moping because you didn't end this right." Sandra leaned forward, toward Melanie. "There are so many unanswered questions. Now that I've had time to think about it, I remember both Chuck and Winston being surprised to see Daphne. It doesn't seem like she was a girlfriend they didn't want us to know about, but more like someone who wasn't expected because she didn't have much significance. Did you consider that, too?"

"That theory would hold true, if you didn't overlook one important factor," Melanie said. "Winston didn't deny that she was his girlfriend."

"As I said before, now that my emotions aren't flying out of control, I can reflect more clearly. Did we really give him a chance to explain? I have to give Winston some due. He just didn't come across as a man who would two-time and use women. And he really was attracted to you. I think you know that."

"What I do know, Sandra, is that he had ample opportunity to explain during the cruise. I had asked him outright about his love life and he gave me the 'no one of consequence' crap. The woman was pregnant and barely showing. That means as recent as a few months or a few weeks ago, he had been sleeping with her. Daphne was under the impression a relationship still existed. All of that adds up to 'someone of consequence.' He should have been open with me."

"That's your pain talking, Melanie," Sandra said in irritation. "You're rationalizing to ease your wounds. Consider the short time you had together and what you did during that time. If it were me, I wouldn't have wasted those few precious moments talking about a dip named Daphne. But I think he would have eventually mentioned her. Call him and find out." Sandra slid the card across the table in front of Melanie.

"Enough, Sandra," she snapped. "Don't piss me off. You're guessing, and I'm not going to put my heart on the line because of a wrong guess. I'm upset, and I don't want to discuss this! Just leave it alone."

"Let me ask you one last thing." Sandra was stubborn. "If Winston showed up right now to talk, would you give him a chance to explain? I think he deserves a chance."

"If Winston showed up right now, it would mean that you had stuck your nose into my business again, because the only way he would show up is if you had told him where I am," Melanie continued. "And if that happened, I wouldn't be as understanding as I was the last time." Melanie stood. "Go dancing tonight if you want, I have work to do."

"That hurt, Mel," Sandra said to her back as Melanie headed down the hall. "You're hitting below the belt."

Melanie stopped. "Life hurts, Sandra." She turned to leave. "I need to call in to my answering machine at home. Try to have a nice day at work."

"I'll see you later." Sandra looked down at the business card on the table. She picked it up and headed to the kitchen trashcan. Opening the lid, she dumped it in.

Melanie's friendship was too important to her. She wouldn't do anything to risk losing it. If her best friend wasn't going to take any steps to resolve her issues with Winston, why should she? Sandra had tried as much as she could.

Winston's business card brought back images of the fun they had had aboard the *Paul Gauguin*. She had enjoyed being around both Winston and Chuck. Maybe she should call and invite Chuck out for drinks. He was a man she wouldn't mind having some fun with again. And if he played his cards right, she might give him a chance to really get to know her.

On the way out the front door heading to the hospital, Sandra made a decision on how to improve her options for a Friday night outing.

"Hey, Sandra! How are you? I got your message to call."

"Chuck, I'm good," Sandra said, standing at the hospital's nurses' station. "I would be better if you were interested in joining me for a drink tonight."

"Sure," he said. "It'll be good to see you. How's Melanie?"

"Surviving."

"You know, what happened in LA wasn't supposed to happen."

"Save it, Chuck. I'm not interested in reliving that. I acted like a fool. I want to apologize for my behavior. You didn't deserve that."

"Crazy situation," Chuck agreed. "But Winston wants to apologize to Melanie for it."

"Well Winston *should* apologize to her. Look, Chuck. That's not my business and I'm staying out of it."

"I hear you," Chuck said. "You said something about treating me to a drink?"

"Like hell I did, but let's meet and I'll see if you deserve one."

Hours later, Sandra came rushing in the house suggesting she and Melanie go out for dinner and drinks, and to her surprise Melanie had just finished packing. She asked Melanie to reconsider. When she refused, Sandra offered to take her to the airport.

"No, I'll take a cab."

The cab ended up being the best solution. It gave them the last hour to reminisce as Sandra got dressed without having to rush or change her plans.

At the front door, Melanie turned and hugged her friend. "I didn't mean to snap at you earlier. Thanks for not letting me get away with it."

"But you're leaving because of it."

"No," Melanie corrected her. "I'm leaving because it's time I faced reality. I need to get my life back on track."

"You know you can come back if you need a friend close by."

"I'll call if I do," Melanie promised. "I'm going to finish my articles, do some research for next year's trip and start preparing for next semester."

"Don't work too hard, Mel."

"Working is what I do best." That was the truth, Melanie thought. It was time to start anew.

Twenty minutes later Sandra strolled into one of the many fancy restaurants in the Addison area. Addison was a short distance from Dallas and was well known for its great restaurants. She had showered and changed into a form-fitting dress. She would miss having Melanie around and still felt she was the cause of her friend's sudden return home. Tonight would help to lift her spirits.

Sandra spotted Chuck sitting in the bar area and headed his way. He stood and hugged her before they sat.

"You look great, Sandra. That dress sure fits in all the right spots."

"You blew your chance with me?" Sandra reminded him, looking for the bartender. "We're at the drinking and buddy status for right now."

"Don't be that way," Chuck laughed. "Let me make it up to you!"

"Not a chance." Sandra placed her purse on the bar and looked around at all the after-work mingling going on around. "But go ahead and try. I'd like to see you grovel."

"Do you think Melanie would let *me* grovel?"

Sandra spun around and looked into a set of sexy eyes that couldn't hide their sadness quickly enough from her. "Winston? I didn't know you'd be here."

"Chuck invited me."

Sandra reached for her purse. "Before I leave, there are few nasty things I want to say to you both. You won't like any of them, but I sure will."

"That's why I'm here," Winston said. "I wanted to apologize to you."

"For what?" Sandra asked. "The airport scene? Hurting my friend? Not telling Melanie about Daphne? Breaking your promise to me? Pick one."

"All of the above," Winston replied. "But mostly for not getting a chance to correct Daphne's lie."

"Lie?" Sandra asked then looked at Chuck.

"Listen to him," Chuck said. "This is why he's here."

Sandra listened intently as Winston explained the details. Then he said, "I don't have a way of contacting Melanie so I can tell her. You're my only chance. She might not listen, but I have to try."

"She won't listen. And I won't help you," Sandra turned to Chuck. "Lose my number. I don't appreciate you playing this game. I told you I was not going to be a part of this."

Winston reached for Sandra's arm. "Let me walk you out."

Outside Sandra said, "Don't waste your time, Winston. If Melanie's not returning your calls, I can't make her."

"I haven't called her. I don't have her number and it isn't listed. She's not at the college this semester and they aren't giving out home information, of course. I can't find her on the Internet; my travel agent got nothing from the cruise line." Winston let out a long sigh. "Do you think I wouldn't be here now, if she didn't matter? I need to see her, Sandra."

"You've been busy, haven't you?" Sandra smiled warmly. "When I find a man who'd do everything you've done just to apologize, I'm going to marry him."

"Tell me how to get to her," Winston pleaded.

"I can't," Sandra said. She opened her car door and stood there. "Melanie would never forgive me if I did. She's hurting and attacks whenever I bring this thing up. If I force this, I'll lose her friendship. I think the two of you should probably talk this out, but she doesn't. She asked that I not tell you how to find her, and I won't break that promise."

Winston did the one thing he had said he would never do again: Manipulate a situation involving Melanie to his advantage.

"What exactly did she say to you?" Winston asked. "It's all in what she asked you to do. Maybe you can keep your promise to her and still allow me to find her."

"Manipulation won't work on me," Sandra said, getting behind the wheel of the car. She started the engine. "I haven't heard one good reason why I should risk losing my best friend."

"I'm in love with her," Winston said simply.

24

Stepping out of the cab at the airport, Melanie looked up. The Dallas evening sky was breathtaking with its array of colors. She had taken pictures of some of these sunsets from Sandra's backyard. Sandra, she thought. Her friendship was as golden as that evening sun. Melanie regretted taking her frustrations out on her best friend. It was time she left, before it happened again.

It wasn't that Melanie was overemotional; only that Sandra was pressing too hard this morning. And Melanie knew she needed to be by herself to consider what was best for her without being rushed.

I need more time.

Melanie got in the long airport check-in line. She debated whether she should check her messages one last time to see if she had gotten an update on her articles. They would either call her or send an email. She had checked her emails before leaving Sandra's but there was no update. She checked her watch. She had over an hour to waste and could use it more constructively than standing in line. If there was an update, she could spend the rest of her airport and flight time working.

If Melanie had planned better, she would have brought her cellular phone and had calls to her home forwarded to it. She sighed and went to find a pay phone.

She had three messages. The first was an approval on an article outline. That lifted her spirits a little. Smiling, she hit the button for the next message. The sound of Winston's deep voice transported her back to the loving days she had had with him in Tahiti. Back to when he had been perfect and she had been happy.

His message: "Melanie, if you delete this message before I'm done, you'll never know how sorry I am for hurting you. I can't change the past week, but I would give anything to erase the memory of the pain it caused you. It bothers me that I can't, but Daphne knows you're the woman I want. The wonderful news is that my sister is the only Knight that's having a baby. Not me. And if it's a boy, she wants to name him Matthew Winston. Poor child." Winston laughed softly, and Melanie found herself laughing with him. His message continued: "If I have to call a hundred times to finish this message I will. I need you, Melanie. I have this void that has grown since I let you slip away from me. And I have this ache because I couldn't prevent you from getting hurt.

"I don't know what I need to do or say to get you back. But I do know that if I don't, my life will be empty. I had forgotten what happiness could feel like, until you came along. The week with you made up for so many years of not having it. I don't want to do this without you..."

There was a long silence and in that space of time Melanie whispered, "I don't want to do this without you either."

Winston's message started again, "And I...." The message abruptly stopped.

Melanie pressed the phone to her ear attempting to hear more. Had it ended or had he hung up? Did he want to say more to her?

Melanie reached for her purse to get his business card and realized she had trashed it. She needed to call him. Where was Sandra? She needed to get his card! Maybe he was in the phonebook? Or maybe had a physician's answering service that could beep him? She reached for the phonebook in the booth where she sat.

The automated voicemail said in Melanie's ear that she had one more message. She had forgotten about that. Fumbling with the phonebook, she managed to press the play key.

The last message started, "This is my second call. I have ninety-eight more times to call you, Melanie. I would prefer telling you what I would say in those messages in person, but if you force me to leave them, I will. You have my work number on the card. But call me at home." He left his home number.

Good God, she pleaded, *why am I crying!* Melanie thought as she hung up. Grabbing her suitcase, she wheeled it away. She needed to leave here.

Winston stood at his patio door, looking out at two empty chairs. In the morning, he would sit on one of those chairs and remember how empty his life was. Turning, he looked at the telephone wondering what time it would ring tonight.

Sandra told him Melanie's plane was in the air and that she wouldn't get home for another few hours.

It took a lot of arm-twisting with Sandra, but in the end he was able to get Melanie's home number. Now the trick was convincing Melanie that Sandra hadn't broken her promise. Sandra really didn't give him any address information. So, her promise of not giving information about Melanie's location was still intact. It was a weak excuse at best, but Sandra had left thinking her promise wasn't broken. At least Winston had gotten her to agree with him that it wasn't.

Weak, he thought, *at best.*

Winston had removed his blazer, shoes and socks. It would be a few more hours before Melanie would get his message, and who knows how long before she returned his call. Unbuttoning his shirt, he figured he would change into something comfortable and relax with a glass of wine.

Maybe he should tell her about all the things he had gone through attempting to find her. It had softened Sandra. Turning to head upstairs to his bedroom, the doorbell rang.

Great, he thought, *Chuck is here*. Someone to talk to.

Opening the front door, Winston wanted to shout, but he stood silently basking in Melanie's smile.

"I was at the airport," Melanie said softly. "Then I thought of the one place I'd rather be. It's here with you."

"How did you find me?" It was the only thing Winston could think to say to her wonderful statement.

"It's seems by the message you left me that I never really lost you."

Winston stepped outside and grabbed her suitcase. "Come in. Please," he said softly. After closing the door behind her, he said, "I was just thinking about you."

Melanie stepped close to him and reached to touch his chest. She rubbed warm pleasurable sensations through his skin, to his heart. "I've missed you."

"I..." Winston looked down at the soft hand wiping away the ache from his heart. "I've missed you more." He looked at the suitcase and said, "I hope you're planning on staying awhile."

"You said you had ninety-eight more messages you wanted to give me. I thought I would stay to hear them all."

"Promise not to leave until I'm done?" he asked.

"Not until I've heard the very last one." She stepped into his arms and wrapped hers around him.

"Okay," he said softly. "I figure you might need a few more outfits to wear. I'm planning to give you about two messages a year. And since you promised to stay with me until I'm done, we may have to go shopping."

Laughing, she said, "Winston Knight, I love the way you manipulate me." Stretching up she pressed a slow, meaningful kiss to his lips. When he moaned, she deepened the kiss.

25

Weeks later, Dallas

Melanie's final article on Polynesia:

"Floating on a Dream" By Melanie McDae

Have you ever awakened from a dream and realized you hadn't been sleeping? It's like that when you take a relaxing cruise around the Society Islands of French Polynesia. The islands are ancient volcanic rock, covered with lush tropical foliage, whose mountainous peaks reach high toward smiling blue skies. But the real secret you'll discover upon arriving is that what you thought were high mountains on Earth are actually low valleys of heaven. My dream vacation started with a pendant the size of a coin that launched a wish for love. Before I had made mine, I thought making wishes were fanciful ideas that added courage to children's doubts. Now, I'm positive they're the things that could help adults rekindle their strengths. Mine went something like this….

Melanie sat reviewing her final article as the early morning sun smiled down on Dallas. In the three weeks she had been with Winston, they had traveled to Colorado once, so she could pick up critical research materials, her laptop, more clothes and to give her plants away to friends. Winston had invited her to stay in Dallas for as long as she wanted; his plan was for her to never leave.

His home was large enough for them to have separate offices to work out of but Melanie opted for using her laptop in different parts of the house, especially the patio. He had a beautiful home, decorated with calming colors. His backyard was a gardener's dream. Trees, shrubs, a water fountain and a gazebo could be seen from the covered patio.

Melanie also found a local entertainment paper she could work for and contacted other national magazines about featuring her articles; including a magazine she found on the plane from Tahiti. The surprising thing, she had discovered, was that when you focused on making your dreams happen, they came to fruition. The more she looked for opportunities to write the more she found. Teaching had been a wonderful opportunity and she would probably do it again some day, but the one important thing she had wanted to do was happening in a short period of time. And she had Winston to thank for that.

However, waking up to Winston each morning was a much better joy that she never wanted to end. Every time Winston woke up and saw her there his response was intensely moving. He really did need for her to love him, and his positive response to her attention made doing so that much more wonderful.

As she sat on his patio typing on her laptop, he stepped out onto the patio carrying a cup of fresh coffee. He sat the coffee next to her and bent to greet her kiss. He was wearing dress pants with a complimenting shirt and tie. It was time for him to head to the office, but he always spent his mornings with Melanie on the patio.

"Good morning," he said looking over her shoulder at the computer laptop's screen. "How's the article coming this morning?"

"I just started it." She smiled as Winston sat next to her. "It's for the magazine *Life&Love*. It's going to be about love and romantic getaways."

"Promise to read it to me when it's done?" he asked.

"Absolutely," she smiled.

"I have something from my last romantic getaway that I want to share with you." He placed a small, black velvet box on the table in front of her."

"Winston?" Melanie whispered, picking up the box. "Jewelry comes in boxes like this."

"Open it," he said softly.

She gently picked up the box with both hands and pressed it to her heart. She looked at him for a long moment. Standing, she moved to sit in his lap. As one hand held the box, the other caressed his face. If eyes were truly the windows to a person's soul, Winston's soul compelled her to love him more. What she saw was a depth of emotion that called to her spirit and warmed her heart.

When Melanie opened the box, she realized her hands were trembling. Inside sat the most beautiful ring she had even seen. A large misty black pearl lay in the center of a bed of diamonds surrounded with a band of gold.

"It's so beautiful," she finally said.

"Let me help you," Winston offered. He removed the ring from her left hand and slid his gift of love onto her finger.

"It's perfect," she whispered as his hand held hers.

"It's you," Winston said. "Will you wear it for me for the next fifty or so years?"

Melanie clasped his face with both hands and kissed him solidly. "Yes," she said softly before leaning against him so she could feel all of him. "I knew it would be like this," she whispered.

"Did Mrs. Hightower tell you about the ring?" Winston grinned.

"No," she said, sitting up so she could look into his eyes. "Can I tell you what I said the first time I saw you?"

He smiled widely. "I've been wanting to know that for a while."

She pulled out the pendant the size of a nickel that was hidden inside the satin, yellow housecoat she wore. It was made of gold with tiny strings of gold wavy lines connecting the sides. "I had to buy this after I had seen you." She pointed to the lines. "Those shapes resemble a man and woman about to kiss."

"I remember when you put that around your neck in the airport," he said. "I couldn't stop staring at it. Or you."

Melanie closed her hand around the pendant and pressed it against her chest. "I placed it around my neck and told Sandra I was going to make a wish. I did. Then I opened my eyes and saw you."

"What did you wish for?"

"To fall in love with a man who would want me to love him."

"Was it that obvious that I needed someone?" Winston asked, laughing.

"No," Melanie said reaching around him. "I didn't realize until you kissed me that you were the man I wished for."

"Melanie," Winston sighed. He kissed her temple before laying his cheek against her hair. He tightened his hold on her, his newfound reality. "I've been living a dream from the moment you kissed me back. I'm going to love you for the rest of my life. I promise."

Dear Reader,

Welcome to my dream....

Cruising the French Polynesian Islands had been a dream of mine for several years. As a writer, I'm allowed to use a little creative freedom, but the notes and information in this novel about the islands are true. Dr. Michael Poole has conducted scientific research on whales and dolphins since 1980. He resides in French Polynesia and does provide lectures and dolphin excursions throughout that area. He visited the ship m/s Paul Gauguin, but unfortunately I did not have the opportunity to meet him in person while abroad.

The m/s Paul Gauguin is a luxury liner of Radisson Seven Seas that serves Tahiti and the other islands of Fre nch Polynesia. To find out more about this ship and others in the Radisson fleet, visit their website: `http://www.rssc.com`.

Winston and Melanie were inspired as I visited the many islands, met with the natives and experienced the joy of a luxury cruise. I thought to myself: What if two people came to French Polynesia for business but found pleasure instead? What you've just read was the result of that spark of an idea. Melanie's damaged spirit could only be appreciated by a sincere man, like Winston, whose soul was looking for a wonderful place to dwell. He found that place in Melanie's heart.

About the Author

Dorothy Elizabeth Love's 4-star novels spark conversation. She's known for writing memorable characters, intriguing plots with wonderful endings. She is also a motivational speaker who teaches workshops on developing and improving the art of writing. She has self-published an instructional guide for aspiring writers called "Putting the Pep in Plotting" which outlines the basics for developing a novel from scratch. Writing is her passion.

Answers to Frequently Asked Questions

Why do you write?

I have this unyielding belief that love can conquer just about all. This is why I enjoy writing stories which depict issues affecting African Americans yet always have a sprinkle of that wonderful ingredient called "romance." My goal is to provide a form of entertainment that allows readers to transcend their current situation, if only for a moment— to be pleasantly entertained and emotionally moved. Although I write to entertain, I also believe in awareness. So social issues that impact African Americans are also addressed in my novels. My characters are flawed yet constantly strive to overcome their imperfections, like most of us, just enhanced a little.

I'm addicted to writing just as much as I'm hooked on enjoying life. I look forward to the day that I can write full-time. For now I'll continue consulting with technology companies and traveling internationally. I was born and raised in Florida, have lived in both North and South America, love cats and am eagerly looking for the next place to move to. The good part about my traveling experiences is that they're fueling my new line of novels.

My first novel was published in 1999. Since then, I've completed over eight novels, three short stories, a self-help guide for aspiring writers, and outlined a dozen other manuscripts.

What would you like your readers to take away from your book?

I write a variety of stories. My first two novels (*Whispers in the Night & And Then Came You*) dealt with more serious issues that affect African Americans. The new TLC Series gives me, and hopefully my readers, a chance to explore the lighter side of life. These novels are designed to cuddle the reader's senses and highlight an exotic place. I hope readers enjoy a small chance to escape into a romantic fantasy, possibly learn something about the human spirit, as well as discover a romantic place to visit using books in this line, such as *Everlasting Moments, When Dreams Float,* and the next release *Crossing Paths, Tempting Memories.*

What are the challenges for you, when building your story line and plot?

My major challenge is not plotting as such but rather the lack of time to fully devote to writing. Managing a fulltime consulting career with travel leaves little time for creative writing. I spend a significant amount of time developing the main characters. In doing so, these characters are so 3-dimensional that, believe it or not, they help me to "tell the story." I want to write because they're as real and close to me as friends or family. Having the time to visit with them is just as difficult as seeing my real friends and family.

How does a story develop for you in going from idea to manuscript?

I start with a memorable or problematical experience I've had then ask a few questions about it. For example: If I tripped and stumbled out of the elevator and into a group of people dropping my notes to an important meeting then I would laugh then ask myself: "What if my female character stumbled into the man of her dreams. He helps her up, but accidentally (or purposely) takes with him the important notes that she was to present at a meeting?" I give the two main characters a profession and a past. And the story starts with my asking five more questions: "How will they first meet?" "When will the first kiss take place?" "Where will the lovemaking happen?" "What will ruin the relationship for them?" and lastly "How will they overcome their issues?"

Do you lean on personal experience, when developing your novel?

Very much so, both the good and the bad. I don't write a story that ?tells all? but I take a small yet impacting piece of something that happened in my life and write a story around it.

Do you find ethnic romances are reaching the cross section of the market, as you would like? Or do you feel limited, as far as in the romance genre?

The leaps and bound African American novelists, in general, have accomplished in the last decade are incredible. Romance is just one more avenue for our voice. Since majority of all books being sold is in the Romance genre, the ethnic variety will soon be in the spotlight. Large publishing houses are also expanding their lines to include ethnic novel. Time is the only thing left to overcome.

Many writers start books, but have trouble finishing. How did you finish your books?

I start with a memorable or problematical experience I've had then ask a few questions about it. For example: If I tripped and stumbled out of the elevator and into a group of people dropping my notes to an important meeting then I would laugh then ask myself: "What if my female character stumbled into the man of her dreams. He helps her up, but accidentally (or purposely) takes with him the important notes that she was to present at a meeting?" I give the two main characters a profession and a past. And the story starts with my asking five more questions: "How will they first meet?" "When will the first kiss take place?" "Where will the lovemaking happen?" "What will ruin the relationship for them?" and lastly "How will they overcome their issues?" I don?t start writing until I've outlined the plot and main characters. This gives me a general idea of how I plan to finish the novel. What that allows is a road map for helping me to get to ?The End? without major difficulty. I find plot sketching extremely helpful since I don't have a lot of time to write. The concepts I use, I put in a how-to guidebook that I give out to writers. Visit the ?For Writers? page on my website, www.DorothyElizabethLove.com, to get a copy.

A consistent routine is key. Carve out uninterrupted writing time and stick to the schedule. For example, writing 2 pages a day will yield a 300-page novel in 5 months.

Do you have any advice for those aspiring writers?

I start with a memorable or problematical experience I've had then ask a few questions about it. For example: If I tripped and stumbled out of the elevator and into a group of people dropping my notes to an important meeting then I would laugh then ask myself: "What if my female character stumbled into the man of her dreams. He helps her up, but accidentally (or purposely) takes with him the important notes that she was to present at a meeting?" I give the two main characters a profession and a past. And the story starts with my asking five more questions: "How will they first meet?" "When will the first kiss take place?" "Where will the lovemaking happen?" "What will ruin the relationship for them?" and lastly "How will they overcome their issues?" Writing is something you have to want to do. For a very few, the first sale is an easy, extremely enjoying, and financially successful experience. But that's not the case for all. So determine what minimum level of success you are willing to accept so that you aren't disappointed.

In terms of writing, visit my website for my helpful writer's guidebook. It will give you ideas of how to outline and sketch out the plot of a novel. Too much writing without a plot sketch can be a time-waster. I put together this guidebook to help aspiring writers gain from my own experiences. Currently, it's free. It's helpful. It's yours for the asking.

Lastly: "Love the desire to write" and "write the story you love."

Excerpt

Someone to Love
By
Alicia Wiggins

July 2003

The bride and groom ran from the reception hall to the waiting limousine as a light snow began to fall and well-wishers shouted their congratulations. It was four weeks before Christmas and the festive spirit of the holiday coupled with that of the wedding filled the air with gaiety, love, and romance.

But Claudia wasn't feeling any of that. As the car pulled away she watched the newlyweds waving excitedly from the open window. The limousine turned the corner and was out of sight. Claudia slipped the wedding souvenirs into her purse-a tiny plastic bottle of bubbles, chocolate kisses, and a miniature gold bell. She would go home and place these items with the countless other wedding souvenirs she'd accumulated over the past year.

Claudia thought about her friend Lorna who that day had just married the man of her dreams. She remembered when Lorna first met Troy. According to Lorna, it was love at first sight. Even though she was hesitant to admit it, that's how it appeared to Claudia as well. The same thing happened when her friend Tracy met her husband Gary.

They had met on a business trip. There was an instant attraction and the two of them clicked. Initially they kept in touch via email and telephone and visited each other whenever they had a free weekend. Soon the strain of maintaining a long-distance relationship became an obstacle that they needed to overcome. Gary was hopelessly in love with Tracy and she with him. They didn't want to lose each other. He eventually put in for a job transfer to Ohio and after a year and a half, the two of them were married. The last time Claudia heard from Lorna, they were expecting a baby.

True love. Must be pretty nice if you could find it, thought Claudia. Even her brother Frank, the interminable bachelor, seemed to have been bitten by the love bug and had a steady girlfriend. Claudia hadn't met her, but if she liked Frank, she had to be special.

Claudia had had enough of the wedding festivities. She looked around for her friend Ray. The two of them had come to the wedding together but now it was time to go and Ray was nowhere to be found.

Claudia sighed. She wanted to be home, soaking in a hot bubble bath and reading a sinfully steamy romance. The last thing she wanted to do was to have to track down Ray.

Looking around the reception hall Claudia spotted Ray across the room talking with their minister. As she walked over to them she noticed two women at a nearby table openly admiring Ray. Claudia didn't blame them. Despite the fact that he was her best friend she had to admit, Ray was pretty nice to look at. There had even been a time or two that she'd found herself wondering what would happen if their friendship ever took a romantic turn. But almost as quickly as she had that thought, she dismissed it. Ray was her friend and good friends were too hard to come by. She could never jeopardize what they had for a romantic fling.

2003 Publication Schedule

Month	Title	Author	ISBN
January	**Twist of Fate**	Beverly Clark	1-58571-084-9
	Ebony Butterfly II	Delilah Dawson	1-58571-086-5
February	**Fragment in the Sand**	Annetta P. Lee	1-58571-097-0
	Fate	Pamela Leigh Starr	1-58571–115-2
March	**One Day at a Time**	Bella McFarland	1-58571-099-7
	Unbreak my Heart	Dar Tomlinson	1-58571-101-2
April	**At Last**	Lisa Riley	1-58571-093-8
	Brown Sugar Diaries & Other Sexy Tales	Delores Bundy & Cole Riley	1-58571-091-1
May	**Three Wishes**	Seressia Glass	1-5871-092-X
	Aquisitions	Kimberly White	1-58571-095-4
June	**When Dreams Float**	Dorothy E. Love	1-58571-104-7
	Revelations	Cheris F. Hodges	1-58571-085-7
July	**The Color of Trouble**	Dyanne Davis	1-58571-096-2
	Someone to Love	Alicia Wiggins	1-58571-098-8
August	**Object of His Desire**	Artiste C. Arthur	1-58571-094-6
	Hart & Soul	Angie Daniels	1-58571-087-3

(Continued on next page.)

2003 Publication Schedule (continued)

Month	Title	Author	ISBN
September	**Erotic Anthology— Fantastist Collection**	(various)	1-58571-113-6
	A Lark on the Wing	Phyliss Hamilton	1-58571-105-5
October	**Angels Paradise**	Janice Angelique	1-58571-107-1
	I'll be your Shelter	Giselle Charmichael	1-58571-108-X
November	**A Dangerous Obsession**	J.M. Jeffries	-58571-109-8
	Just an Affair	Eugenia O'Neal	1-58571-111-X
December	**Shades of Brown**	Denise Becker	1-58571-110-1
	By Design	Barbara Keaton	1-58571-088-1

Other Genesis Press, Inc. Titles

A Dangerous Deception	J.M. Jeffries	$8.95
A Dangerous Love	J.M. Jeffries	$8.95
After the Vows (Summer Anthology)	Leslie Esdaile *and* T.T. Henderson *and* Jacqueline Thomas	$10.95
Again My Love	Kayla Perrin	$10.95
Against the Wind	Gwynne Forster	$8.95
A Lighter Shade of Brown	Vicki Andrews	$8.95
All I Ask	Barbara Keaton	$8.95
A Love to Cherish	Beverly Clark	$8.95
Ambrosia	T.T. Henderson	$8.95
And Then Came You	Dorothy Elizabeth Love	$8.95
A Risk of Rain	Dar Tomlinson	$8.95
Best of Friends	Natalie Dunbar	$8.95
Bound by Love	Beverly Clark	$8.95
Breeze	Robin Hampton Allen	$10.95
Cajun Heat	Charlene Berry	$8.95
Careless Whispers	Rochelle Alers	$8.95
Caught in a Trap	Andre Michelle	$8.95
Chances	Pamela Leigh Starr	$8.95
Dark Embrace	Crystal Wilson Harris	$8.95
Dark Storm Rising	Chinelu Moore	$10.95
Designer Passion	Dar Tomlinson	$8.95
Eve's Prescription	Edwina Martin Arnold	$8.95
Everlastin' Love	Gay G. Gunn	$8.95
Fate	Pamela Leigh Starr	$8.95
Forbidden Quest	Dar Tomlinson	$10.95
From the Ashes	Kathleen Suzanne Jeanne Sumerix	$8.95
Gentle Yearning	Rochelle Alers	$10.95
Glory of Love	Sinclair LeBeau	$10.95
Heartbeat	Stephanie BedwellGrime	$8.95
Illusions	Pamela Leigh Starr	$8.95
Indiscretions	Donna Hill	$8.95
Interlude	Donna Hill	$8.95
Intimate Intentions	Angie Daniels	$8.95
Kiss or Keep	Debra Phillips	$8.95
Love Always	Mildred E. Riley	$10.95
Love Unveiled	Gloria Greene	$10.95
Love's Deception	Charlene Berry	$10.95

Other Genesis Press, Inc. Titles (continued)

Mae's Promise	Melody Walcott	$8.95
Meant to Be	Jeanne Sumerix	$8.95
Midnight Clear (Anthology)	Leslie Esdaile *and* Gwynne Forster *and* Carmen Green *and* Monica Jackson	$10.95
Midnight Magic	Gwynne Forster	$8.95
Midnight Peril	Vicki Andrews	$10.95
My Buffalo Soldier	Barbara B. K. Reeves	$8.95
Naked Soul	Gwynne Forster	$8.95
No Regrets	Mildred E. Riley	$8.95
Nowhere to Run	Gay G. Gunn	$10.95
Passion	T.T. Henderson	$10.95
Past Promises	Jahmel West	$8.95
Path of Fire	T.T. Henderson	$8.95
Picture Perfect	Reon Carter	$8.95
Pride & Joi	Gay G. Gunn	$8.95
Quiet Storm	Donna Hill	$8.95
Reckless Surrender	Rochelle Alers	$8.95
Rendezvous with Fate	Jeanne Sumerix	$8.95
Rivers of the Soul	Leslie Esdaile	$8.95
Rooms of the Heart	Donna Hill	$8.95
Shades of Desire	Monica White	$8.95
Sin	Crystal Rhodes	$8.95
So Amazing	Sinclair LeBeau	$8.95
Somebody's Someone	Sinclair LeBeau	$8.95
Soul to Soul	Donna Hill	$8.95
Still Waters Run Deep	Leslie Esdaile	$8.95
Subtle Secrets	Wanda Y. Thomas	$8.95
Sweet Tomorrows	Kimberly White	$8.95
The Price of Love	Sinclair LeBeau	$8.95
The Reluctant Captive	Joyce Jackson	$8.95
The Missing Link	Charlyne Dickerson	$8.95
Tomorrow's Promise	Leslie Esdaile	$8.95
Truly Inseperable	Wanda Y. Thomas	$8.95
Unconditional Love	Alicia Wiggins	$8.95
Whispers in the Night	Dorothy Elizabeth Love	$8.95
Whispers in the Sand	LaFlorya Gauthier	$10.95
Yesterday is Gone	Beverly Clark	$8.95
Yesterday's Dreams, Tomorrow's Promises	Reon Laudat	$8.95
Your Precious Love	Sinclair LeBeau	$8.95

Featured Poem

Come Down, Heaven

by Joyce Hudson

As the stars settle in the heavens
For their nocturnal watch
I will await the rapture of your love
A love that so deftly
Touches my heart
Sweetly enticing my soul to come hither
To be wrapped in the beauteous wonder
Of you
A love so willing to lay itself open
Like blossoms before me
Enveloping me with
Their musky fragrance
A love that shines like the stars
That look down upon us
Twinkling their approval of our sweet embrace
A love that alights my ear
With soft refrains
Sweetly dissipating into every part of my soul
A love that witnesses our unity
And binds us with perfection
Unifying our souls into one
A love that floods
Rains of spring
Burns
Heat of summer
A love that surpasses
Colors of autumn
And warms an Arctic winter day
One love that deliciously brings forth
A sweet nectar from your lips
When they touch my own
May heaven shine its approval down upon us
As I imbibe every part of
Your love

ORDER FORM

Mail to: Genesis Press
315 3rd Avenue North
Columbus, MS 39701

Name ____________________

Address ____________________

City/State ____________________ Zip ____________

Telephone ____________________

Ship to (if different from above)

Name ____________________

Address ____________________

City/State ____________________ Zip ____________

Telephone ____________________

Qty.	Author	Title	Price	Total

Use this order form or call 1-800-INDIGO-1	Total for books:	______
	Shipping and handling:	
	$5.00 first two books.	
	$1.00 each additional:	______
	Total amount enclosed:	______
	Mississippi Residents add 7% sales tax	

Visit www.genesispress.com for latest releases and excerpts

ORDER FORM

Mail to: Genesis Press
315 3rd Avenue North
Columbus, MS 39701

Name ______________________________

Address ______________________________

City/State ______________________ Zip ____________

Telephone ______________________

Ship to (if different from above)

Name ______________________________

Address ______________________________

City/State ______________________ Zip ____________

Telephone ______________________

Qty.	Author	Title	Price	Total

Use this order form or call 1-800-INDIGO-1	Total for books:	______
	Shipping and handling:	
	$5.00 first two books.	
	$1.00 each additional:	______
	Total amount enclosed:	______
	Mississippi Residents add 7% sales tax	

Visit www.genesispress.com for latest releases and excerpts

ORDER FORM

Mail to: Genesis Press
315 3rd Avenue North
Columbus, MS 39701

Name ______________________________

Address ______________________________

City/State ____________________ Zip ______________

Telephone ______________________

Ship to (if different from above)

Name ______________________________

Address ______________________________

City/State ____________________ Zip ______________

Telephone ______________________

Qty.	Author	Title	Price	Total
Use this order form or call 1-800-INDIGO-1	Total for books: Shipping and handling: $5.00 first two books. $1.00 each additional: Total amount enclosed: *Mississippi Residents add 7% sales tax*			

Visit www.genesispress.com for latest releases and excerpts